The Secret of Ella and Micha

Jessica Sorensen

Borrowed Hearts Publishing

For information:

http://jessicasorensensblog.blogspot.com/

Cover Design by Mae I Design and Photography
www.maeidesign.com

The Secret of Ella and Micha
ISBN 9781939045010

Prologue

Ella

I wonder if I can fly? With the wind and rain in my hair and my arms out to the side of me, it feels like it might be possible. Perhaps if I can get enough courage to jump off the thin ledge, I'll soar away into the night, like a bird with powerful wings.

Maybe then I could reunite with her.

"What are you doing?" Micha says, his voice higher than normal. "Get down from there. You're going to hurt yourself." His aqua eyes pierce me through the rain and his hands are on the beams above his head, hesitant to climb out onto the ledge.

"I don't think I will," I say. "I think I might be able to fly... just like her."

"Your mom couldn't fly." He balances onto the railing and glances down at the murky water far below our feet. "What are you on?"

"I took one of her old pills." I tip my head back and bask my face in the rain. "I just wanted to see what it was like for her. Why she thought she was invincible."

He steps down on the beam with his arms spanned out to the side and his clunky boots slip on the wet metal. The lightning flashes above our heads and collides with the earth.

"Your mother didn't know better, but you do." Bracing one hand on the metal wire above our heads, he extends his other hand toward me. "Now come over here. You're scaring the shit out of me."

"I don't know if I can," I say softly, raising my head back up as I rotate to face him. "I'm not sure if I want to."

He dares a step closer and his thick eyelashes blink fiercely against the down pour. "Yes, you do. You're stronger than that." His hand begs me closer. "Please, just get over here."

Staring down at the black water, my body starts to drift.

"I swear to God, Ella!" Micha shouts, his tone sharp, his muscles tense. "Give me your hand!"

I snap out of my daze and tangle my fingers with his. His other hand captures my waist and he leads us swiftly back to the railing, lifting me over it. My feet settle onto the concrete of the bridge that is pooled with puddles. Lights on the beams illuminate the night and Micha's car is parked in the middle of the bridge with the driver's door open and the engine and headlights on.

He hops over the railing and then his arms are around me, embracing me securely, like he's afraid to let go. For a second, it feels okay, weightless and uncontrolled. I tuck my face into his chest, the wet fabric damp against my chilled skin. The scent of him takes me to a place I wish I could go back to—my childhood. Back when things weren't as heavy because I was too immature to grasp the full reality of life.

Micha pulls back and smoothes my wet hair out of my eyes. "Don't you ever do that to me again. I can't do this without you."

But he needs to figure out life without this perception of me, because I don't know how long I can keep doing it without drowning.

"Micha, I..." The look on his face silences my lips.

He knows what I'm about to say—he always does. He is my best friend, my soul mate. In a perfect world, full of roses and sunshine we'd be together, but this world is full of broken homes, drunken fathers, and mothers who give up easily.

"I'm sorry." I cling to him as I say my final good-bye. "I didn't want to think anymore. It was just too much and my mind wouldn't slow down. But it's alright now. I can think clearly again."

He cups my cheek, his thumb searing hot as he traces the pad lightly across my cheekbone. "Next time come to me—don't just run. *Please.* I know things are hard right now, but it'll get better. We've always made it through every single bad thing thrown at us." Beads of water trickle in his eyelashes, along his cheeks, over his full lips. There's a shift in the air, one I've felt coming for a long time.

His lips part. "Ella, I love—"

I crush my lips against his, hushing him and melting our bodies together. I allow his tongue to caress mine, letting him suck the rain from my bottom lip and savor the taste of me. We arc into each other, like we can't get enough and heat flows through our drenched clothes, warming my skin. I could let it go on forever, but that would be wrong.

The girl he thinks he loves needs to disappear. I don't want tonight to be irreversible, so I pull away, breathing him in one last time. Then I walk away, leaving him on the bridge in the rain, along with the old Ella.

Chapter 1

8 months later...

Ella

I despise mirrors. Not because I hate my reflection or that I suffer from Eisoptrophobia. Mirrors see straight through my façade. They know who I used to be; a loud spoken, reckless girl, who showed what she felt to the world. There were no secrets with me.

But now secrets define me.

If a reflection revealed what was on the outside, I'd be okay. My long auburn hair goes well with my pale complexion. My legs are extensively long and with heels, I'm taller than most of the guys I know. But I'm comfortable with it. It's what's buried deep inside that frightens me because it's broken, like a shattered mirror.

I tape one of my old sketches over the mirror on the dorm wall. It's almost completely concealed by drawings and obscures all of my reflection except for my green eyes, which are frosted with infinite pain and secrets.

I pull my hair into a messy bun and place my charcoaled pencils into a box on my bed, packing them with my other art supplies.

Lila skips into the room with a cheery smile on her face and a drink in her hand. "Oh my God! Oh my God! I'm so glad it's over."

I pick up a roll of packing tape off the dresser. "Oh my God! Oh my god!" I joke. "What are you drinking?"

She tips the cup at me and winks. "Juice, silly. I'm just really excited to be getting a break. Even if it does mean I have to go home." She tucks strands of her hair behind her ear and tosses a makeup bag into her purse. "Have you seen my perfume?"

I point at the boxes on her bed. "I think you packed them in one of those. Not sure which one, though, since you didn't label them."

She pulls a face at me. "Not all of us can be neat freaks. Honestly, Ella, sometimes I think you have OCD."

I write "Art Supplies" neatly on the box and click the cap back on the sharpie. "I think you might be on to me," I joke.

"Dang it." She smells herself. "I really need it. All this heat is making me sweat." She rips some photos off her dresser mirror and throws them into an open box. "I swear it's like a hundred and ten outside."

"I think it's actually hotter than that." I set my school work in the trash, all marked with A's. Back in High School, I used to be a C student. I hadn't really planned on going to college, but life changes — people change.

Lila narrows her blue eyes at my mirror. "You do know that we're not going to have the same dorm when we come back in the fall, so unless you take all your art-work off, it's just going to be thrown out by the next person."

They're just a bunch of doodles; sketches of haunting eyes, black roses entwined by a bed of thorns, my name woven in an intricate pattern. None of them matter except one: a sketch of an old friend, playing his guitar. I peel that one off, careful not to tear the corners.

"I'll leave them for the next person," I say and add a smile. "They'll have a predecorated room."

"I'm sure the next person will actually want to look in the mirror." She folds up a pink shirt. "Although, I don't know why you want to cover up the mirror. You're not ugly, El."

"It's not about that." I stare at the drawing that captures the intensity in Micha's eyes.

Lila snatches the drawing from my hands, crinkling the edges a little. "One day you're going to have to tell me who this gorgeous guy is."

"He's just some guy I used to know." I steal the drawing back. "But we don't talk anymore."

"What's his name?" She stacks a box next to the door.

I place the drawing into the box and seal it with a strip of tape. "Why?"

She shrugs. "Just wondering."

"His name is Micha." It's the first time I've said his name aloud, since I left home. It hurts, like a rock lodged in my throat. "Micha Scott."

She glances over my shoulder as she piles the rest of her clothes into a box. "There's a lot of passion in that drawing. I just don't see him as being some guy. Is he like an old boyfriend or something?"

I drop my duffel bag, packed with my clothes, next to the door. "No, we never dated."

She eyes me over with doubt. "But you came close to dating? Right?"

"No. I told you we were just friends." But only because I wouldn't let us be anything more. Micha saw too much of me and it scared me too much to let him in all the way.

She twists her strawberry blonde hair into a ponytail and fans her face. "Micha is an interesting name. I think a

name really says a lot about a person." She taps her mani-
cured finger on her chin, thoughtfully. "I bet he's hot."

"You make that bet on every guy," I tease, piling my
makeup into a bag.

She grins, but there's sadness in her eyes. "Yeah,
you're probably right." She sighs. "Will I at least get to see
this mysterious Micha—who you've refused to speak
about our whole eight months of sharing a dorm together—when I drop you off at your house?"

"I hope not," I mutter and her face sinks. "I'm sorry,
but Micha and I… we didn't leave on a good note and I
haven't talked to him since I left for school in August."
Micha doesn't even know where I am.

She heaves an overly stuffed pink duffle bag over her
shoulder. "That sounds like a perfect story for our twelve
hour road trip back home."

"Back home… " My eyes widen at the empty room
that's been my home for the last eight months. I'm not
ready to go back home and face everyone I bailed on. Especially Micha. He can see through me better than a
mirror.

"Are you okay?" Lila asks with concern.

My lips bend upward into a stiff smile as I stuff my
panicked feeling in a box hidden deep inside my heart.
"I'm great. Let's go."

We head out the door, with the last of our boxes in our hands. I pat my empty pockets, realizing I forgot my phone.

"Hold on. I think I forgot my phone." Setting my box on the ground, I run back to the room and glance around at the garbage bag, a few empty plastic cups on the bed, and the mirror. "Where is it?" I check under the bed and in the closet.

The soft tune of Pink's "Funhouse" sings underneath the trash bag—my unknown ID ringtone. I pick up the bag and there is my phone with the screen lit up. I scoop it up and my heart stops. It's not an unknown number, just one that was never programmed into my phone when I switched carriers.

"Micha." My hands tremble, unable to answer, yet powerless to silence it.

"Aren't you going to answer that?" Lila enters the room, her face twisted in confusion. "What's up? You look like you just saw a ghost or something."

The phone stops ringing and I tuck it into the back pocket of my shorts. "We should get going. We have a long trip ahead of us."

Lila salutes me. "Yes, ma'am."

She links arms with me and we head out to the parking lot. When we reach the car, my phone beeps.

Voicemail.

Micha

"Why is Ella Daniels such a common name," Ethan grunts from the computer chair. His legs are kicked up on the desk as he lazily scrolls the internet. "The list is freaking endless, man. I can't even see straight anymore." He rubs his eyes. "Can I take a break?"

Shaking my head, I pace my room with the phone to my ear, kicking the clothes and other shit on my floor out of the way. I'm on hold with the main office at Indiana University, waiting for answers that probably aren't there. But I have to try—I've been trying ever since the day Ella vanished from my life. The day I promised myself that I'd find her no matter what.

"Are you sure her dad doesn't know where she is?" Ethan flops his head back against the headrest of the office chair. "I swear that old man knows more than he's letting on."

"If he does, he's not telling me," I say. "Or his trashed mind has misplaced the information."

Ethan swivels the chair around. "Have you ever considered that maybe she doesn't want to be found?"

"Every single day," I mutter. "Which makes me even more determined to find her."

Ethan refocuses his attention to the computer and continues his search through the endless amount of Ella Daniels in the country. But I'm not even sure if she's still in the country.

The secretary returns to the phone and gives me the answer I was expecting. This isn't the Ella Daniels I'm looking for.

I hang up and throw my phone onto the bed. "God Dammit!"

Ethan glances over his shoulder. "No luck?"

I sink down on my bed and let my head fall into my hands. "It was another dead end."

"Look, I know you miss her and everything," he says, typing on the keyboard. "But you need to get your crap together. All this whining is giving me a headache."

He's right. I shake my pity party off, slip on a black hoodie, and a pair of black boots. "I've got to go down to the shop to pick up a part. You staying or going?"

He drops his feet to the floor and gratefully shoves away from the desk. "Yeah, but can we stop by my house. I need to pick up my drums for tonight's practice. Are you going to that or are you still on strike?"

Pulling my hood over my head, I head for the door. "Nah, I got some stuff to do tonight."

"That's bull." He reaches to shut off the computer screen. "Everyone knows the only reason you don't play

16

anymore is because of Ella. But you need to quit being a pussy and get over her."

"I think I'm going to... " I smack his hand away from the off button and squint at a picture of a girl on the screen. She has the same dark green eyes and long auburn hair as Ella. But she has on a dress and there isn't any heavy black liner around her eyes. She also looks fake, like she's pretending to be happy. The Ella I knew never pretended.

But it has to be her.

"Dude, what are you doing?" Ethan complains as I snatch my phone off my bed. "I thought we were giving up for the day."

I tap the screen and call information. "Yeah, can I get a number for Ella Daniels in Las Vegas, Nevada." I wait, worried she's not going to be listed.

"She's been down in *Vegas*." Ethan peers at the photo on the screen of Ella standing next to a girl with blonde hair and blue eyes in front of the UNLV campus. "She looks weird, but kinda hot. So is the girl she's with."

"Yeah, but she's not your type."

"Everyone's my type. Besides, she could be a stripper and that's definitely my type."

The operator comes back on and she gives me a few numbers listed, one of the numbers belongs to a girl living on the campus. I dial that number and walk out into the hall to get some privacy. It rings and rings and rings and then Ella's voice comes on the voicemail. She still sounds the same, only a little unemotional, like she's pretending to be happy, but can't quite get there.

When it beeps, I take a deep breath and pour my heart out to the voicemail.

Chapter 2

Ella

"I swear to God if we don't find a bathroom soon, I'm going to piss in my pants." Lila bounces up and down in the driver's seat. The air conditioner is turned up as high as it will go and "Shake it Out" by *Florence + The Machine* plays from the speakers. There's a long road of highway stretched out in front of us, weaving over the hills spotted with trees, sage brush, and the pale pink glow of the sunset.

My cell phone is in my pocket, heavy like it weighs a hundred pounds. "You can always pull over and pee behind a bush." I prop my bare feet up on the dash and pull my white lacy tank top away from my skin to get air flowing. "Besides, we're like five minutes away from the offramp."

"I can't hold it for five more minutes." She shoots me a dirty look and squeezes her legs together. "You're not going to think it's so funny when the car smells like piss."

I smother a laugh and search the GPS for the nearest restroom. "There's one right off the exit, but I think it's more of an outhouse."

"Does it have a toilet?"

"Yes."

"Then it works." She makes a sharp swerve, cutting off a silver Honda. The Honda lays on its horn and she turns in her seat to flip him the middle finger. "What a jerk. Doesn't he understand that I have to pee?"

I shake my head. I love Lila to death, but sometimes she can be a little self-centered. It's part of what drew me to her; she was so different from my old friends back in Star Grove.

My phone beeps again for the millionth time, letting me know I have a message waiting for me. Finally, I shut it off.

Lila turns down the music. "You've been acting weird ever since we left. Who called you?"

I shrug, gazing out at the grassy field. "No one I want to talk to right now."

Five minutes later, we pull up to the outhouse at the edge of town. It's more like a shack with rusty metal siding and a faded sign. The field behind it is spotted with corroded cars and trucks and in front of it is a lake.

"Oh thank God!" She claps her hands and parks the car. "I'll be right back." She jumps out and shuffles inside the bathroom.

I climb out of the car and stretch my legs, trying not to look at the lake or the bridge going over it, but my gaze magnetizes toward the level bridge with beams curving overhead and out from the sides. The middle one was where I was standing the night I almost jumped. If I squint one eye and tilt my head, I can spot it.

An old Chevy pickup comes flying down the road, kicking up a cloud of dust. As it nears, my nose twitches because I know who it is and he's one of the last people I want to see. The truck stops just outside the perimeter of the field behind the restrooms. A lanky guy, wearing a tight t-shirt, a snug pair of jeans, and cowboy boots comes strutting out.

Grantford Davis, town pothead, infamous brawl starter, and the guy who dropped me off at the bridge that God awful night eight months ago.

I bang on the bathroom door. "Come on Lila, hurry up."

Grantford looks my way, but there's no recognition in his eyes, which isn't surprising. I've changed since the last time anyone saw me, shedding my gothic clothes, heavy

21

eyeliner, and tough-girl attitude for a more lighter and pleasant look, so I blend in with the crowd.

"You can't rush nature, Ella," Lila hisses through the door. "Now let me pee in peace."

I watch Grantford like a hawk as he rolls a tire across the field toward his pickup.

The bathroom door opens and Lila walks out cringing. "Gross, it was so disgusting in there. I think I might have caught herpes just looking at the toilet." She shivers, wiping her hands on the side of her dress. "And there were no paper towels."

Grantford has disappeared, although his truck is still there.

I grab Lila's arm and tug her toward the car. "We need to go."

Lila elevates her eyebrows questioningly as she tries to keep up with me. "What's wrong with you?"

"Nothing," I say. "There was just this guy over in the field that I *really* don't want to talk to."

"Is he an old boyfriend?"

"No, not even close...." I trail off as Grantford rounds the bathroom.

There's sweat on his forehead and grass stains on his jeans. "I need to talk to you for a minute."

"Why?" I question, swinging the car door open. *Please don't bring up that night. Please.*

Lila freezes as she's opening the door and her gaze darts to me. "Ella, what's going on?"

Grantford tucks his hands into his pockets, staring at the hood of the car. "This ain't your car, is it?"

"No, we just stole it and took it for a joy ride." Shit. Ten minutes back and my old attitude is slipping out. "I mean, yes it is—her car anyway." I nod my head at Lila.

"Well, I was just wondering how fast it goes?" He gives me a fox smile that makes me want to gag.

I was never a fan of Grantford. He always had a sleazebag attitude, which was part of the reason why I had him drive me to the bridge that night—he was the only one I knew who would leave me there alone.

I can't help myself. "Probably a lot faster than your pick up over there."

He has a shit-eating grin on his face. "Is that a challenge?"

I shake my head and motion for Lila to get in the car "Nope, that wasn't a challenge. Just a mere observation."

Recollection fills his eyes. "Wait a minute. Do I know you?" Ignoring him, I start to shut the door, but he catches it. "Holy crap! I do know you. You're Ella Daniels." His eyes mosey up my legs, cutoff jeans, lacy white tank top, and land on my eyes lined with frosty pink eyeliner. "You look... different."

"College will do that to you." I scale up his scuffed cowboy boots, his torn jeans, and stained shirt. "You haven't changed a bit."

"I see your mouth hasn't changed at all," he snaps. "And besides, you didn't change for the better. In fact, you look like you could be friends with Stacy Harris."

"Don't exaggerate the situation," I say. Stacy Harris was a popular girl in our grade; head cheerleader, homecoming queen, wore a lot of pink.

His face scrunches. "You didn't just change on the outside either. If anybody would have compared you to Stacy Harris, you'd have punched them in the face."

"Violence solves nothing." I begin to shut the door again. "I have to go."

He complements my move and seizes the door, prying it back open. "You ain't going anywhere until I get something out of you."

"Like a kick to the balls," I threaten, but my insides churn. I can talk tough, but when it all comes down to it he's a really big guy who could easily hurt me.

His grey eyes turn black as the sun sets behind the shallow hills. "I heard you bailed. Packed up your stuff one night and took off. Pissed off a lot of people, too. The ones that were always protecting you when that mouth of yours got you into trouble. Especially that one guy you were always with."

24

"Don't pretend like you don't know his name." My voice is slightly uneven. I feel out-of-control of the situation and I'm starting to panic. "You don't forget the names of the people whose fist have slammed into your face."

A vein bulges in his thick neck as he punches the window. "That night, I was wasted and Micha was completely sober. And it was total bull shit that he sucker punched me for leaving you on the bridge. I mean, you asked me to take you there. How the hell was it my fault?"

Apparently, Micha hit him more than once because it's not the instance I'm referring to.

I tug at the door handle. "I'm going to close the door now and you're going to walk away."

"Who are you?" His eyes are all over me.

"I'm who I always was," I mutter. "Just without all the baggage." Calmly, I close the door. "You can drive away now, Lila."

She floors the car backwards and skids it onto the asphalt. I don't look back at Grantford or the bridge. I breathe through my nose, trying to stay composed and in possession of my feelings.

"What was that about?" Lila asks. "Who was that creep?"

I buckle my seatbelt and turn up the air conditioning. "Just some guy I used to know from high school."

"I thought he was going to kill you or something...
Maybe we should call the police."

Flashbacks of my old life resurface. "That's just how
things are around here. Besides, he was all bark and no
bite. Trust me. He was just irritated with something I did."

Her eyes enlarge and she grips the steering wheel.
"What did you do?"

I glance in the rearview mirror at the desolate road
behind us. "Nothing I want to talk about."

She slows down as the speed limit decreases. "How
did you do that? You were so calm even when he tried to
hold the door open. *I* was freaking out."

"It was just instincts," I lie. If she knew the real reason
we sure as hell wouldn't be friends.

***

The urge to make Lila flip a U-turn and floor it back to Vegas becomes more powerful the closer we get to my home.
Lila relaxes about the Grantford ordeal when the outhouse
is far behind us. We make the rest of the short drive talking about classes and frat parties, but when we pull into
the driveway of my house, her fear and panic reemerges.

"This is... nice." She shudders as she peers through
the windshield. "So this is where you grew up?"

The full moon shines in the starry sky, lighting up the
trash piled in the driveway, the old cutlass balanced on

cinderblocks in front of the garage, and the peeling paint off my two-story home trimmed with a broken rain gutter that's swaying in the wind. The tree beside my window looks like it's dying. It was once my gateway for sneaking out of my room, but the last time I snuck out was the night my mother died.

I'll never climb that damn tree again.

"Yep, this is home." I step out into the cool breeze. *Rise Against* "Like an Angel" blasts from the speakers next door. The lights are on in the house, and there's a lot of screaming and yelling going on. The driveway is lined bumper to bumper with cars and people are smoking on the dry front lawn and on the deck.

One of Micha's parties. It's like time has frozen and was waiting for me to return.

"God things never change around here." I round the back of the car. "Lila, can you pop the trunk, please."

The trunk pops open and Lila steps tentatively out of the car. Her eyes fasten on the party and she's chewing on her thumbnail, which is a nervous habit of hers. "Jeez, it's more intense than even a frat party. I didn't know that could be possible."

I sling a heavy bag over my shoulder. "Are you sure you want to sleep at my house tonight?" I rummage through the trunk for the bag holding all my toiletries.

"There are some pretty decent hotels in the next town over."

"I'm just not used to this kind of a place. That's all... But I'm sure it's fine." She collects one of my pillows from the trunk and hugs it tightly.

"Are you absolutely sure?" I balance a small box under my arm. I don't want her to stay and witness this side of my life. "This place is a lot to take in for some people."

She narrows her eyes and points a finger at me. "I may come from an upper class town, but that doesn't mean I haven't been in rougher areas before. Besides, we went to that pawn store that one time in Vegas and that neighborhood was definitely sketchy."

It really wasn't that bad of an area, but I decide to let it go, since she'll only be staying here for one night.

"Sorry, I just... I want to make sure you're comfortable." I shift the bag onto my hip and feel around the dark trunk for my other bag.

"I promise I can manage for one night." She crosses her heart with her finger and smiles. "In fact, I might even get brave enough to go check out the party next door."

I rapidly switch the subject. "We can probably get the rest of this stuff out tomorrow, since it's dark and I can barely see. And I don't know about you, but I'm exhausted."

"I think…" Her eyes wander in the direction of the driveway. "Dear God Almighty, who is *he*? Wait a minute. Isn't he… yeah…" She lets out a quiet squeal and hops up and down. "Ella, I think it's the guy from your drawing, that Micha guy you insist you never dated."

My bag falls to the ground as I slouch down, debating an escape. *Duck under the car? Run into the house? Dive into the trunk?*

"Hey there, beautiful," Micha says in his flirty tone. "You shouldn't park your car out here in the open. Someone will probably jack it."

The sound of his voice sends a tremble through my body that coils down deep inside me. I thought the feeling would be gone after being away for eight months, but somehow time has had the opposite effect—it's amplified and taking over my body. I pretend to be engrossed by a box in the trunk and put my head amidst the shadows.

Lila giggles. "I'm sure my car will be okay. This is my friend's house."

"Your friend's house…" He drifts off, making the connection and anxiety strangles me. "Wait a minute? Are you talking about Ella Daniels?"

Collecting myself, I slam the trunk down. When he sees me, his eyes enlarge and he has the same expression on his face as when his mama told him his daddy wasn't ever coming back.

He blinks the stunned expression away and a hint of anger transpires. "What are you doing here? I thought you were in Vegas."

For a moment, I'm unable to speak, caught in a mixture of emotions from seeing him again. Micha has always been stunningly beautiful in a way that makes artists' hands ache. He's dressed in a red plaid shirt, dark jeans, and a pair of black boots. His lips are full and ornamented with a silver loop and his dirty blonde hair has a slight wave to it. His skin is like porcelain and his aqua eyes carry more than I can handle.

"I was down there for school, but I'm back now," I say in the polite tone I've used with everyone over the last eight months. But on the inside my heart is wild, and my blood is roaring with the same yearning I felt for him when I left. "Wait a minute. You knew I was down there?"

He sidesteps around Lila and positions himself directly in front of me. Micha is one of the few guys that is taller than me and I have to angle my head up to meet his eyes. "I had no idea where you were until this morning," he says. "Since you didn't tell anyone where you went."

The ache in his voice stabs at my heart and the phone carrying the voicemail in my pocket weighs a thousand pounds. "Sorry, but I needed a break from this place. It was... things were... well you know how it was."

30

"No, I don't know how it was." He braces a hand on the trunk like he's going to fall over. "Since you took off and never told me where the hell you went."

I need to go before he gets to me, and all my self-control evaporates. Picking up my bag from the ground, I wave good-bye to him. "It was nice talking to you again, but we've been on the road for like twelve hours and all I want to do is lay down."

"I'm not really that tired," Lila says and I press her with a pleading look. "Oh, wait maybe I am." She fakes a yawn.

I hurry for the side door of my house, but Micha blocks my path, and his hand comes down on the car like a railroad track barricade. He drags his lip ring into his mouth with a passionate look on his face, like he might kiss me or something.

For a second, I wish he would.

He leans toward my ear, lowering his voice to an intimate level. "Come with me somewhere. *Please*. I've been waiting eight months to talk to you."

I flinch at my body's fiery reaction his voice emits. "I can't talk to you, Micha." I choke, backing away, and bumping my hip on the edge of the car. Tears threaten the corners of my eyes, but I haven't cried in over a year and I refuse to break down. Spinning on my heels, I dash for the house.

He doesn't call out to me—it's not his style. But his gaze bores a hole into my messed up head the entire way, until I'm finally locked inside my house.

Then I can breathe again.

Micha

I swear I'm dreaming. Ella is standing in front of me and she looks just like Stacy Harris, a slutty cheerleader we used to go to high school with and who Ella beat up once because Stacy was making fun of a girl in a wheelchair.

It was one of the things that made me fall in love with her; the fire, passion, and the need to stick up for the outcasts, even if it meant being an outcast herself. She never fell into any category—she was just Ella—but now she looks like a freakin' Stepford Wife. She's still hot as hell, a rock hard body, and long legs that go on forever. I've pictured those legs wrapped around my waist many times and the same images flood my head, even though she looks like a stranger.

Her gorgeous green eyes are glossed over, like she's repressed everything inside. She's unhappy to see me and it hurts a little, but pisses me off more. She starts rambling about being tired, something she used to do all the time to avoid confrontation. I watch her lips move, wanting to kiss her so God damn bad, but knowing she'd probably kick me if I tried anything. So I lean in, smelling her hair and beg her to come with me somewhere.

Then she runs down the driveway and locks herself in the house. I start to chase after her, but a Frisbee smacks me in the side of the head.

"Sorry man," Ethan calls out, hopping over the fence with a smirk on his face. "It slipped."

Rubbing my head, I arch my eyebrows at Ethan. "Perfect timing asshole."

He holds up his hands. "I said I was sorry. You were just standing there all dazed out like a freaking whipped pussy, so I thought I'd snap you out of it." He scoops up the Frisbee from the concrete and gives a low whistle at Ella's friend's Mercedes as he circles it rolling up his sleeves. "Whose sweet ride is this? Wait, is it Ella's?"

"I think it's her friends." I eye the back door of her house, debating whether I should barge in after her and demand to know why she shut me out for eight months.

"Since when does Ella hang out with people who drive cars like this?" he asks, peeking through the tinted windows.

"She's been gone for eight months." I back toward the fence that separates Ella's yard from mine with my hands in my pockets. "Who the hell knows who she is anymore?"

I need a drink, even though I haven't had a drop of alcohol in eight months. The day Ella took off, with no note or a good-bye, I had gone up to the cove, got drunk, and took all my anger out on Grantford Davis' face. The cops showed up and I got busted for being under the influence and for assault. I'm still on probation for it and I had to go to anger management classes for a while. I've been really good about keeping my crap together, but five minutes after Ella shows up and I'm about to throw it away.

I head to the kitchen, scoop up a beer from the ice chest, and settle on the couch between a blonde and a brunette.

The blonde one giggles. "Oh my God, is the bad boy Micha finally back?"

I can't remember her name, but I play along. "I sure am, baby."

Then I swig my beer back and bury my pain, along with Ella. She's the only girl that's ever been able to get me this upset. The only girl that's never wanted me.

Chapter 3

Ella

"I take it that's Micha?" Lila wanders around my kitchen as she tightens a loose ribbon on the waist of her floral dress. "He's even cuter than in the picture."

"Yep, that would be Micha." I kick a box across the stained linoleum floor and flip the light on. It looks the same; seventies themed colors, wicker chairs around the glass table, and yellow and brown countertops.

"So just your dad lives here?" Lila circles the small kitchen and her gaze lingers on the countertop next to the kitchen sink where empty bottles are lining the wall.

"Yeah. My older brother moved out as soon as he graduated." I adjust the handle of my bag and head for the stairway. The house smells like rotten food and smoke. In the living room, the aged plaid sofa is vacant, and the ash tray on the coffee table is spilling over with cigarette butts. The television is on so I shut it off.

"So where's your dad?" Lila wonders as we climb up the stairs.

"I'm not sure," I avoid the truth, because he's probably at the bar.

"Okay, where's your mom?" she probes. "You never told me where she lives."

Lila doesn't know much about me and it's how I want it. Leaving her in the dark, about my mom, my brother — everyone in this aspect of my life — has allowed me to transform into someone who doesn't have to deal with my problems.

"My dad works nights," I make up a story. "And my mom moved out quite a while ago. She lives up on Cherry hill."

She leans forward to study a portrait of my mother displayed on the wall; the same auburn hair, pale skin, and green eyes as me. Her smile was just as fake as mine, too. "Is this your mom?" She asks and I nod. "She looks just like you."

My chest tightens and I quickly trot to the top of the stairway. At the end of the hall, the bathroom door is wide open. The corner of the porcelain tub and the stain on the tile floor is in my line of vision. My heart constricts tighter as the memories flood me. I'm suffocating with panic.

"Baby girl," she said. "I'm going to go take a nap, just for a little while. I'll be back in just a bit."

My knees tremble as I shut the door. My chest opens up and oxygen flows through my lungs again.

"So where does your brother live?" Lila peers inside my brother's room full of drums, guitar picks, CDs, and records. There's a bunch of band posters taped to the wall and a guitar up on a mount.

"I think in Chicago."

"You think?"

I shrug. "We don't have the best relationship.

She nods, like she understands. "So is he in a band?"

"I'm not sure if he's still in one now. I'm guessing since his stuff's here, probably not," I say. "He only played because he was friends with Micha and he's in a band. Or was. I have no idea what he does anymore."

"Ella, did you lose touch with everyone in your life?" Lila accuses, tucking the pillow under her arm.

Her scrutiny makes me uncomfortable. Avoiding confrontation, I turn on my bedroom light and shudder at the sight. It's like a museum of my past. Sheets of my artwork are tacked to the walls, trimmed with a black skeleton border Micha put up when we were twelve to make my room more "manly." A collection of guitar picks line the far dresser and there is a pile of my boots in the corner. My bed is made with the same purple comforter and there's a plate with a half-eaten cookie on it, which is growing mold.

I toss the cookie into the trash. Hasn't my dad been in here since I left?

Lila picks up a guitar and plops down on the bed. "I didn't know you played." She positions the guitar on her lap and strums the strings. "I always wanted to learn how to play, but my mom would never let me take lessons. You should teach me."

"I don't play." I drop my bag on the floor. "That's Micha's guitar. His initials are on the back."

She turns it over and looks at the initials. "So the hot guy from next door is also a musician. God, I'm about to swoon."

"No swooning over anyone in this neighborhood," I advise. "And since when are you into musicians? I have never, until today, heard you say anything about liking guys who can play the guitar."

"Since they look like him." She points over her shoulder toward Micha's house, which is visible through the window of my room. "That boy is dripping with sexiness."

Jealousy growls in my chest and I mentally whisper for it to shut up. I pick up a photo of my mom and me at the zoo when I was six. We're happy, smiling, and the sun is bright against our squinting eyes. It rips at my heart and I let the photo fall back onto the desk. "There's a trundle under the bed that you can sleep on if you want."

"Sounds good." She slides the guitar off her lap and goes over to the window, drawing the curtain back. "Maybe we should go to the party. It looks kind of fun."

I gather my hair away from my eyes before dragging the trundle out from under the bed. "No offense, Lila, but I don't think you can handle one of Micha's parties. Things can get a little bit crazy."

She narrows her eyes at me, insulted. "*I* can handle parties. It's you that never wanted to go to any of them. And the one's that I did talk you into going to, you just stood in the corner, drinking water and sulking."

I flop down on the bed with my arms and legs slack over the edges. "That party is nothing like a college frat party. They're the kind of parties you wake up from the next day on a park bench with no shoes on and a tattoo on your back, with no recollection of what happened the night before."

"Oh my God, is that how you got that tattoo on your back—the one you refuse to tell me what it means." She lies on the bed next to me and we stare at the *Chevelle* poster on my ceiling.

"It means infinite." I tug the hem of my tank top down, hiding the tattoo on my lower back, and drape my arm over my forehead. "And I don't refuse to talk about it. I just can't remember how I got it."

She gives me a sad, puppy dog face and bats her eyelashes. "Pretty please, with a cherry on top. This might be my only chance to go to a party like this. The ones at my old neighborhood consist of limos, fancy dresses and tuxes, and a lot of champagne." When I don't respond, she adds, "You owe me."

"How do you figure?"

"For giving you a ride here."

"Please don't make me go down there," I plead, clasping my hands together. "*Please.*"

She rolls onto her stomach and props up on her elbows. "He's an old boyfriend, isn't he? You were lying. I knew it. No one can draw a picture like that of someone they've never loved."

"Micha and I have never dated." I insist with a heavy sigh. "If you really want to go see what these parties are all about, I'll take you down there, but I'm not hanging around for more than five minutes." I give in because deep down I'm curious to check up on the world I left behind.

She claps her hands animatedly and squeals, looking out the window one last time. "Holy crap. Someone's standing on the roof."

They say curiosity killed the cat. "Come on, party girl. Let's get this over with."

***

40

About fifteen years ago, this town used to be a decent place to live. Then the factory that supplied jobs to almost the entire town shut down. People were laid off and slowly it began to dwindle into the bottomless pit that it is now. The houses across the street are painted in graffiti and I'm pretty sure my next door neighbor makes moonshine in his garage, or at least he did before I left.

Inside Micha's house, there are people loitering in the entryway. I push my way through them and into the kitchen, which is crammed with even more people. On the table is a kegger and enough bottles of alcohol to open a liquor store. The atmosphere is overflowing with the scent of sweat and there are a few girls dancing on the kitchen counters. People are making out in the corners of the living room where the sofas are shoved to the side, so the band can flare on their instruments, screaming lyrics of pain and misunderstanding at the top of their lungs. I'm surprised Micha isn't up there playing.

"Holy crap. This is…" Lila's blue eyes are round as she gawks at the people jumping up and down in the living room, shaking their bodies and thrashing their heads.

"Like a mosh pit," I finish for her, shoving a short girl with bleached hair out of my way.

"Hey," the girl whines as her drink spills down the front of her leather dress. "You did that on purpose."

For a split second, I forget who I am and turn around to blast her with a death glare. But then I remember that I'm the calm and rational Ella; one that doesn't get into fights and beat other girls up.

"What, preppy girl?" She pats her chest, ready to throw down. "You think you scare me."

Lila bites her thumbnail. "We're sorry. She didn't mean to."

Chants fill the living room and the chaos is giving me a headache. "Sorry," I strain an apology and squeeze between her and the wall.

She snickers at me and her friends join in with her laughter as they sashay to the back door. It takes everything I have not to turn around and tackle her to the floor.

Lila makes a beeline for the bar set up on the counter, dumps a drop of vodka into a cup, and mixes it with a splash of orange juice. "Okay, that was intense. I thought she was going to kick your ass."

"Welcome to Star Grove." I shout over the music. "The Land of the Intense and Poverty-stricken, where the adolescents roam free without sober parental supervision and try to start fights wherever they can."

She laughs, takes a gulp of her drink, and her face pinches at the bitterness. "Try—" She starts, then coughs. She pounds her hand against her chest.

"Are you going to make it?" I ask. Lila has never been a big drinker.

She nods and clears her throat. "I was going to say try growing up where you have to get permission to wear a certain style of shoes." I give her a mystified look and she adds, "If it wasn't up to my mother's stylish fashion standards I wasn't allowed to wear it."

I edge out of the way of a guy with blotchy skin and a beanie covering his head, who doesn't seem to mind that he knocks his shoulder into mine. "I'm sure it wasn't that bad growing up where you did. I mean, at least there was some control."

"Yeah, there was," she says uneasily and her eyes quickly scan the room. "I can't believe there's a live band. It's like being at an outside concert."

"What? They don't have live bands in California?" I joke with a small smile as I pour myself a cup of water. "One's that take place outside?"

She stirs her drink with a straw. "Not these kinds of bands. Think much more mellow, with a stage and seats to watch."

"Sounds like fun to me." I oblige a smile and glance at my watch. "Are you about ready to go?"

"Are you joking?" Sucking the drink out of the straw, she hops on the counter and crosses her legs. "We just got here. Why would we want to go? In fact, we should go dance."

My eyes find the living room, where a guy with dreads smashes his head against the glass plate of a cabinet in the corner and everyone cheers.

"You can if you want, but I'm good." I gulp my water. "I like all my bones intact."

Leaning against the counter, I scan through the crowd, curious to see where Micha is. I don't know why I'm so curious, but I am. Occasionally he would bail on his own parties, either to hook up or just get some quiet. I found him a couple of times hiding out on a lawn chair. Each time, he would pull me onto his lap and we would stare up at the night sky, talking about an unreachable future.

I spot him in the corner, sitting on the couch with his arm draped around some blonde girl with boobs popping out of her dress. His hair hangs in his eyes and he's nibbling at his lip ring, driving the girl crazy I'm sure. They're just talking, but the girl keeps flipping her hair off her shoulder and her hand is on his chest. It's hard to tell if Micha's enjoying her company or not. He was always difficult to read when it came to girls because he never really looked interested in any of them, but sometimes he would end up with them for the night.

I asked him about it once and he said it was all fun, but that he was just killing time until I gave into my inner desire to be with him. I tackled him to the ground for it and it made him laugh.

"Why do you have that look on your face? Like you're undressing someone with your eyes?" Lila asks, following my gaze. "Oh, is that—"

My eyes dart from Micha. "I wasn't looking at anyone, just the madness in the living room."

"Yeah, right," she says, elevating her eyebrows. "You totally want him. I can see it on your face."

"Well, I'll be damned if it isn't the infamous Ella May!" Ethan Gregory grins from the other side of the counter, just behind Lila. He stumbles around the corner, nearly clipping his head on the low ceiling. Before I can respond, he has me trapped in an awkward hug with his long arms that are tracked with tattoos. His grey shirt smells like an ash tray and his breath like beer. He pulls back, ruffling his black hair with his fingers. "Does Micha know you're here in his house?"

I lie breezily, very aware of where Micha is and what he's doing. "I'm pretty sure he saw me walk in."

"I doubt that. He's been looking for you for the past eight months." He glances over his shoulder and nods at Lila, then tips in toward me. "You know he's been a wreck ever since you took off. You really fucked up his head, Ella."

"That's such a lie," I tell him. Ethan and I have never really gotten along very well, which is why the hug confused me so much. We both had the same blunt attitude and butted heads a lot. The only reason we were friends at all was because of Micha. Although, there was one time we did bond for a split second, but we never talk about it. "Micha doesn't fall apart over anyone. I know him better than that."

His face is flushed and his brown eyes are bloodshot. "I guess you don't know him as well as you think then, because he's been a wreck. In fact, all he's done for the last few months is search for you."

"Which explains the party," I retort. "I'm guessing that classifies as that."

"First one in five months," he says. "And I think he only did it because he found out where you were and needed a distraction."

"I know him better than you do, Ethan, and he doesn't fall apart over girls," I say, but cringe at the fact that I might not know him anymore. A lot can happen in eight months. "Hey, Lila, we should go. It's getting late."

She glances at her diamond encrusted Rolex and rolls her eyes. "It's like nine thirty."

"You're leaving already?" He waves his hand in the air. "That's nonsense talk right there. You haven't even seen Micha yet and he's gonna be super pissed if he misses

46

seeing you, especially since you ran away from him in the driveway."

"Actually, I think we're going to hang out for a little while longer," Lila presses with unrelenting eyes. She mouths, *he's hot.* Then she fastens her hands together. *Please, Ella. Pretty please.*

Ethan isn't Lila's type. He's got baggage almost as heavy as mine. I start to protest when Micha's deep voice floats over my shoulder and tickles my skin like feathers. Without being able to help it, I let out a soft moan.

"Yeah, pretty girl, stay a little longer." He's so close that the heat of his body kisses my skin and my insides tremor. His fingers comb through my hair as he whispers, "You smell so good. God I've missed your smell."

"I have to get up really early in the morning." I clear my throat and Lila's eyebrows furrow. "I need to go home and get some sleep."

He places his hand on the counter, so the crook of his arm is touching my hip. "You can keep trying to avoid me," he breathes in my ear, taking a nip at my earlobe. "But sooner or later you're going to have to talk to me." His breath reeks of beer and his clothes of smoke.

Refusing to crack at the sound of his sexy voice, I turn and face him. "I don't have time to get drunk and act like a moron."

He's even more gorgeous under the light and more irresistible, even though his eyes are glossed over. "It's your fault I'm drunk—you drive me crazy." He descends his voice to a soft purr, the same voice he's used on me many times to get what he wants—the voice that makes me feel alive inside. "Baby, come on. Please. We need to talk." He leans in to kiss me.

The suddenness throws me off balance and I trip over my own feet. "Micha, stop it." I gently push him back and he staggers into the edge of the counter. "You're drunk. And I'm going home."

"She's acting weird... like she's way too calm," Ethan remarks, with a wave of his finger. "And she's dressed funny, like that girl we use to go to school with. What's her name?" He snaps his fingers. "Stacy.... Stacy..."

"Harris," I say exhausted. "And I look like a girl that went away to college and grew up."

Lila slants forward. "Ella's been this way since I've known her, but I'm really curious what she used to look like with the way everyone keeps talking about her because I can't picture her any other way besides this."

Micha and Ethan trade drunken looks and then howl with laughter. The room quiets down a little as people glance in our direction.

"What's so funny?" Lila frowns and looks to me for help. "I'm so lost."

"Nothing. They just think they're funny." I dodge around Micha, but he seizes my elbow and hauls me back against his chest. "Hey relax, baby." He kisses my forehead and gives me his innocent face. "Please don't go. I just got you back."

Before I took off, the boundaries of our friendship were starting to blur. I thought time would fix this, but it seems like we're back to where we started. As much as I would love to melt into him, it just can't happen. I can't open up like that and lose control. I need control.

"No one's got me back. I'm just here for summer break and only because I didn't have money to rent an apartment," I say and his expression falls. "The Ella you knew is gone. She died on that bridge eight months ago."

He blinks, as shocked as I am. His lips part then he clasps them shut, struck speechless.

"I didn't mean that," I say quickly. "I'm sorry, Micha. I just can't deal with this."

"Don't be sorry for being real," he says, rubbing his forehead with the back of his hand.

I force the lump in my throat down. "I'm sorry," I say again, and then weave through the crowd and out the back door, inhaling the fresh air.

"What's your problem?" Lila asks as she catches up with me at the edge of my driveway. She squashes her plastic cup and tosses it into the trash can on the back porch. "I'm so confused. What just happened?"

"I needed to get out of there before I lost it." I don't slow down until I'm in my room where I close the door and shut the window, locking away the world. I sigh back against the wall, breathing in the quiet.

Lila watches me with inquisitiveness as she pulls her hair back into a bun and puts some lip gloss on. "Ethan and Micha act like you used to be someone else. Like this isn't the real you. Want to explain?"

"Not really." I push away from the door and collect some pajamas from the duffel bag. "I'm going to go take a shower. Do you need anything from downstairs?"

"Yeah, for you to tell me why those guys have you so frazzled." She unclips her watch and tosses it into her purse that's on the bed. "I've never seen you so worked up like that. You basically had an orgasm when you first saw him."

"I did not," I say, embarrassed and annoyed. "And you haven't seen me that worked up because I'm not that person anymore."

"Except for when you're around him," she insinuates. "When you were talking to him, there was something in your eyes I've never seen before. You were always so closed off to all the guys at parties and in school. Honestly, I thought you were a virgin. But the way you and Micha

50

were looking at each other—you've had sex with him, right?"

Pressing my lips together, I tuck my pajamas under my arm, and shake my head. "No, Micha and I've never slept together, just like we've never dated. But we've been friends since we were kids."

She sits down on the bed and unhooks her sandal. "But you've had sex before?"

I squirm in my skin. "I'm going to go get ready for bed."

"*Whoa*, wait a second." She leaps off the bed wearing one shoe and jumps in front of the door with her hands spread out to the side. "Are you saying that you've never had sex? *Ever.*"

I struggle for words she'll understand. "It's not like I haven't because I don't believe in premarital sex or anything. I just… Look there's a lot you don't know about me and sometimes I have a hard time getting close to people."

She's not surprised. "Well, obviously. That's totally been a given from day one."

"What do you mean?" I question. "I've never told anyone that before." *Not even Micha.*

"It means sometimes I can see right through you." She sighs and counts down on her fingers. "I've been your roommate for eight months and all I know about you is you're focused on school, you hate to drink, hate being around large crowds, and have never went on a date. I barely know you and being here, I'm starting to wonder if I know you at all."

She knows the Ella I want her to know. "Can you let me by? I'm really tired."

She gives me a disbelieving look, but doesn't press. She steps aside and lets me by. Relief washes over me because I don't want to get into it with her. Not tonight. Not ever. I never want to get into the night that changed my life. I buried my reckless identity, and I won't dig it up again.

Chapter 4

Micha

"She's already got you all hot and bothered." Ethan sips on his soda. "Look at you. Drunk after eight months of sobriety and I don't believe it's a coincidence it happened on the same night she showed up."

I slam another shot back and wipe my lips with the back of my hand. "I'm fine man. And I can't blame what I do on anyone else but myself. This isn't Ella's fault."

Ethan laughs, tipping his head back, bumping it on the edge of the cupboard. "Who the hell are you trying to convince? You know just as well as every single person in the room knows that you two are each other's problem and it's never going to be fixed until you fuck and get it over with."

I punch him in the arm, harder than I planned. "Watch it. You're walking on thin ice tonight."

He holds up his hands, surrendering. "Sorry, I forgot how you get when you're like this."

I grab a fist full of his shirt and jerk him toward me. "Like what?"

Again, he forfeits up his hands. "Micha man, calm down and go drink some coffee or something. You're trashed out of your mind."

I release him and rake my fingers through my hair, frustrated with something I can't grasp. "Coffee's a myth… And I need something else." My eyes travel to the back door window, and suddenly I understand what I need. I pat Ethan's shoulder. "Clear everyone out before my mom gets home, okay?"

"Alright, man will do," he replies confoundedly. "But where are you going?"

"On a walk." I knock people out of my way, and stumble out the back door. Regaining my balance, I trip across the grass and climb over the fence. Ella's dad's Firebird is parked in the driveway, so he must be home from the bar. Doesn't matter, though. He won't notice or care if I sneak in. I've been doing it since we were kids.

Although, my intentions did get a bit dirtier the older we got.

I stare up at her bedroom window until I reach the tree. After a drunken struggle, I make it to the top and I inch along the branch to the window. Cupping my hands around my eyes, I peek inside. The lights are off, but the glow of the moon lights a trail to her bed. She's fast asleep. I inch open the window, slicing my finger on a rusty nail. "Mother..." I suck on my finger tip, the taste of blood and vodka bitter against my tongue as I head dive through the window and hit the floor with a soft thud.

Her friend shoots upright from the bed on the floor, her eyes wide. "Oh my God."

I put my finger to my lips as I get to my feet. "Shh..." She still looks worried so I dazzle her with my most charming smile.

That seems to win her over and she settles back in her bed. As carefully as I can, I step over her bed and crawl in with Ella. She's always been a heavy sleeper and doesn't stir. I press my chest against her back, drape my arm over her waist, and feel the rhythm of her breathing. God, I've missed this way too much. It's not healthy. I burrow my face in her neck, smelling the scent of her hair, vanilla mixed with something that's only her.

I shut my eyes and for the first time in eight months, I fall into a peaceful sleep.

Ella

I sleep horribly for half the night, tossing and turning, like the princess sleeping on a pea. Only I am far from a princess and the pea is my guilty conscience. I don't know why I feel guilty about blowing off Micha. I've done it breezily for the past eight months. Although, he wasn't living right next door with his sad puppy dog eyes and charming sexiness.

My sleep deprivation only got worse when my dad stumbled into the house in the middle of the night, bumping over cups and bottles, drunk off his ass. Later, I heard him crying in the bathroom my mom died in. It still hurts to hear because his tears are my fault.

Once I fall asleep, I am *out* and it ends up being the best night's rest I've had in ages. When I wake up in the late afternoon, I feel refreshed and calm. Until I realize why.

Micha is in my bed and has me in his long, lean arms. His body is curved into mine, so *every* single part of him is touching me. I know it's him by the smell of his cologne mixed with mint and something else that only belongs to Micha. I pretend to be asleep, engulfed in a wonderful dream, refusing to wake up until he leaves.

"I know you're awake," he whispers in my ear. His voice is hoarse and his breath is stale with booze. "So open your eyes and quit avoiding me."

"You know it's illegal to walk into someone's house without permission," I say with my eyes shut. "And sneaking into someone's bed—that's the move of a pervert."

"I didn't walk in. I fell in," he says, amused. I pinch his firm chest and he laughs. "Now there's my feisty girl." He brushes his soft lips across my forehead. "I've missed you, Ella May."

Opening my eyes, I wiggle in his arms. "Please don't start. It's too early."

His eyes are guarded and his hair is a mess. He chuckles lowly, a sound that ripples deep inside my core. "Pretend all you want, pretty girl. You and I know that deep down you're secretly glad to be pressed up to my body." He urges our chests together as he snakes his legs around mine.

My eyelids flutter against his warmth. God, I've missed this so much. Way too much and so has my body, evidently.

"So where did you go?" he asks, crushing my moment of bliss. "To school in Vegas? Because it kind of surprises me. You never really liked school."

My mind snaps back to reality. "I don't want to get into this right now. I just want to have a relaxing summer and then I'm headed back to campus."

He blinks, his eyelashes fluttering against my forehead. The feel of him sends a warm tingle up my thighs and I seal my lips to keep from moaning.

His eyebrows knit. "It's like you've been kidnapped by a bunch of nuns or something."

"Maybe I was," I say submissively. "It wouldn't hurt anyone if I was."

He considers this and an artful smirk curves at his lip. "That's not true. Nuns can't have sex and I still haven't fulfilled my lifelong dream of having sex with you."

I open my mouth, my tongue locked and loaded with an equally perverted comeback, but I bite down, remembering I'm not that kind of a girl anymore. "I need to wake Lila up. She's got a long drive ahead of her."

With one swift roll, he has me pinned down beneath his body and my arms trapped above my head. His aqua eyes search mine and it's like staring at the endless ocean. He sucks on his lip ring, lost in thought. "You're going to tell me, pretty girl," he asserts, tilting his head so his lips are next to my cheek. "You always tell me everything."

"Micha, please...." I despise how breathless I sound. "You know why I left. You were there that night... you saw me... I can't do it again." Anxiety claws up my throat and my muscles tense beneath the weight of his body. "Please let me up. I can't breathe."

He props up on his arms. "You could have talked to me, instead of running away. You know that."

I shake my head. "No, I couldn't. Not that time. That time it was different. You were part of the reason I had to leave."

"Because you kissed me?" he asks, dipping his voice to a husky growl. "Or because I found you that way... that night."

I swallow the giant lump in my throat. The kiss was part of it. It was an earthshattering kiss, one that stole breaths, stopped hearts, and scared the shit out of me because it surfaced feelings I'd never felt before, ones that rendered me helpless.

"I don't want to talk about it. Now get off of me." I wiggle my arms between us and push on his chest.

He sighs and rolls off me. "Fine, don't talk about it, but it doesn't mean you can run away from me again. I'll chase you down this time," he threatens with a wink as he climbs off the bed, and the chain hooked to his studded belt jingles. "Get dressed and meet me out in the driveway. You have to go visit Grady today."

"No, thanks," I decline and tug the blanket over my head. "And I told you last night I have stuff to do today. Besides aren't you hung over from last night? You were pretty wasted."

"Don't do that," he says, aggravated. "Don't pretend like you have some deep insight into me anymore. You've been gone for eight months and a lot has changed."

I'm speechless. "Micha, I... "

"Come on, get out of bed. You're going to see Grady, whether you like it or not." He yanks the blanket off me and tosses it on the floor, so I'm lying there in my plaid shorts and skin-tight tank top with no bra on underneath. He gives me a prolonged once over, with a dark, lustful glint in his eyes and goosebumps sprout all over my skin.

I cover myself with my arms. "I'm not going to Grady's. I just got home and I have things to do."

"He's got cancer, Ella." He backs for the door, tucking his hands into the pockets of his faded jeans. "So get your bratty, split-personality ass out of bed and go see him before you can't."

My arms fall to my sides as I sit up. "Why didn't anyone tell me?"

"If you would have told someone where you were, we would have," he says. "Although, I'm pretty sure your father knew where you were, he just wouldn't tell anyone."

I don't deny it.

"Besides, I told you in the voicemail I left yesterday," he says, glancing at my phone on the desk. "But I'm guessing you haven't listened to that?"

I shake my head. "No, I was too surprised to see your number on the screen."

He bites on his lip ring, something he does when he's nervous. "Yeah, you should probably just delete that. I don't think you're ready for it yet."

My gaze moves to my phone. What the hell is on it? I climb out of bed, arching my back and stretching like a cat. "How bad is Grady?"

He swallows hard. "He's dying, so you need to get dressed and let me take you to see him."

I begin to object, but rethink my initial stupidity. Grady is the one part of my past that I could never run from. At one point, he was like a father to Micha and me. I even called him from Vegas once, although I didn't tell him where I was.

I nod. "Let me get dressed and I'll be out in a second."

"See you in a few." He winks at me and vanishes into the hall, leaving the door wide open behind him.

Lila quickly springs up from the trundle bed, clutching the sheet. "Oh. My. Hell. What was that about? I mean, he crawled in here through the window in the middle of the night, and just climbed into bed with you."

"That's what he does." I open the window letting in the gentle breeze. Loose pieces of my hair dance around the frame of my face. "Oh, no."

Lila stretches her arms above her head. "What's wrong?"

I reluctantly look at her. "I think someone might have confused your car for a canvas."

She jumps out of bed and elbows me out of the way to get a look at the damage done to her beautiful, nearly brand new Mercedes. "My poor baby!"

I pull a skirt and a pink tank top out of my duffel bag. "Get dressed and we'll go check out the damage."

She pouts, looking like she might cry. "I can't drive it home like that. My parents will kill me."

"I know plenty of people who can fix it for you," I say, opening the door. "Or I use to, but I'm sure it's all the same."

She nods and I go to the downstairs bathroom to change, avoiding the upstairs one. I turn on the shower so the mirror will fog up and hide my reflection. I comb my hair until it flips up at the ends naturally. Then I apply a light shade of lip gloss and head out the door, but run into my dad on the stairway.

"When did you get here?" His breath smells like gin and his eyes are red. His cheeks have sunken in over the last eight months and his skin is wrinkled like leather with sores. He's in his late forties, but looks like he's pushing sixty.

"Last night," I tell him, taking his arm and helping him up the stairs. "I was in bed before you got home."

He offers me a pat on the back. "Well, I'm glad to have you home."

"I'm glad to be home," I lie with a smile as we reach the top of the stairs.

He moves his arm away from my hand and rubs the back of his neck. "Do you need anything? Like help carrying in your boxes?"

"I think I can handle it on my own, but thanks." I decline, sticking my arm out as he teeters toward the stairs.

He nods and his eyes drift to the bathroom down the hall. He's probably thinking about how much I look like her. It hurts his eyes, at least that's what he told me the night I went to the bridge.

"I guess I'll talk to you later then. Maybe we could go to dinner or something?" He doesn't leave me time to answer as he zigzags down the hall to his room, slamming the door shut behind him.

My dad started drinking when I was about six, a few months after my mom got diagnosed with a bipolar disorder. His drinking habit wasn't that bad back then. He would spend a few nights at the bar and sometimes on the weekends, but after my mom died, beer and vodka took over both our lives.

When I return to my room, Lila is dressed in a yellow sundress, with her blonde hair curled up and there is a pair of overly large sunglasses concealing her eyes.

"I feel like crap," she declares, putting her hands on her hips.

"This place has that effect on most people." I grab my phone, noting the flashing voicemail as I slip on my flip flops.

We go outside, leaving the smoky air behind and step into the bright sunlight, surrounded by the scenery of run-down homes and apartments. The neighborhood is filled with motorcycle engines revving and far in the distance are the sounds of a lovers' quarrel and Micha is nowhere to be seen.

A long time ago, it felt like home, back when street racing and running wild felt natural, but now I just feel lost.

Lila starts biting at her fingernails as she gapes confoundedly at her car. "It looks worse up close."

I circle her car with my arms folded, assessing the damage. It looks like a fruit basket, only instead of being filled with fruit it's crammed with innuendos and colorful words. I'm on the verge of laughing for some reason. "They got you good."

She shakes her head. "This isn't funny. Do you know how much it's going to cost to fix this?"

Lila's dad is a big shot lawyer over in California. Her parents are always sending her things like clothes, money, cars. She has never worked a day in her life and gave me a hard time for my waitressing job at Applebee's, begging me to take time off to go to parties.

"So what do we do?" She chips at some green paint on the headlight with her fingernail.

I point up the street. "There's an auto body shop not too far from here."

She glances down the road, which is covered in potholes and lined with filthy gutters. "But this is a Mercedes."

"I'm sure painting a car, no matter who the maker is, is all the same."

"But what if they do something to it?"

"Like spray paint it again after they paint it?" I say sarcastically and she scowls. "Sorry. We'll find someone, okay? We can take it to someplace in Alpine. It's a little nicer over there."

"I can't drive it when it looks like this," she complains, motioning at the car. "It's hideous."

"I'll drive it, then," I offer my hand out for her to give me the keys.

"Are you joking?" She pats the hood of her car. "This is my baby. No one drives it but me. You know that."

"I think your baby is in serious need of some plastic surgery." Micha strides off the porch of his house and onto the driveway. He's changed into black jeans, a fitted grey t-shirt, and his blonde hair hangs in his eyes. Using his long legs, he jumps over the chain-linked fence between our yards. "I know the perfect place to get it fixed and it's here in town, so you won't have to drive it so far." He gives Lila a wink. "I'm Micha, by the way."

"Hi, I'm Ella's roommate or old roommate anyway," she says with a warm smile and slides her sunglasses down the brim of her nose. "We're not sure if we're sharing a dorm room next semester."

He presents her with his player grin. "Sharing a room with Ella? That had to be tough." He shoots me a mischievous look, trying to get a rise out of me.

She laughs and returns her glasses over her eyes. "No, she's a pretty great roommate, actually. She cleans and cooks and everything. It's like having my own house maid."

"Ella was always good at that stuff," he agrees, knowing the real reason why. Even before my mom died, she was never good at taking care of the house. I had to learn how to take care of myself at a very young age, otherwise I'd have starved and rotted away in a rat-infested house. "So do you want me to take your car to that shop I was talking about? Like I said, it's really close."

"Yeah, that sounds great." She shuffles her sandals against the concrete. "I'd rather go someplace close."

I mentally roll my eyes. Leave it to Micha. He can get any woman to contradict herself if he wants to.

He swings his arm around my shoulder and kisses me on the forehead. "But I have to take pretty girl over here to see an old friend first."

"Please stop calling me that," I beg. "I've never liked the nickname and you know that. I never even got why you called me it."

"And that's the appeal of it, pretty girl." He tempts me closer to him and caresses my cheek with his lips, giving me a kiss that brings warmth to my skin. "Now are you ready to go see Grady? You can come, too, if you want… is it Lila?"

"Yeah, it's Lila. Lila Summers." She offers her hand and Micha shakes it. "And sure I'll go. This place makes me a little nervous."

"Isn't your family expecting you to be home tonight?" I escape from underneath Micha's arm.

"I'll text them and tell them I'm not leaving until to-morrow." She retrieves her cell phone and scrolls through her contacts. "The car will be done by tomorrow, right?"

"It's hard to say," Micha says. "Ethan is the best, but a little slow."

Her head snaps up and there's delight in her eyes. "Ethan as in Ethan from the party last night? The one with the sexy hair and the really big hands?"

Micha bites down on his lip, stifling a laugh, and flicks me a sideways glance. I can't help but smile.

"Yep, that's the one," he says. "Do you feel better about taking your car to him now?"

"Well, yeah, if *you* think it's okay?" she checks. "I'm very picky about who works on my car or at least my dad is very picky about who works on it."

"It'll be fine," he assures her with a wink. "I've never disappointed a girl yet."

"Oh yeah?" Lila laughs, glancing at me uneasily, like she's worried she's stepping on my territory.

"So are we going to go or what?" A ping of jealousy pinches inside my chest.

"Yep, let's go, beautiful." Micha leads the way around the fence and up his driveway to the garage.

When I step inside, my mouth falls open. Parked in the middle, between the walls lined with shelves and tools, is a shiny 1969 Chevy Chevelle SS. It's painted in a smoky black with a cherry red racing stripe down the center. "You finally fixed it up?"

He pats the shiny flawless hood, his eyes sparkling with excitement. "I finally got around to it, after talking

68

about it for four years." His eyes find mine, seeking my approval. "So what do you think?"

"It's kind of old." Lila pulls a face at the car. "And really big."

"I thought you liked things big?" Micha teases. I punch him in the arm and he laughs. "Ow, I meant hands. Jeez get your mind out of the gutter."

I roll my eyes. "You did not, you pervert."

He shrugs, his eyes lustrous in the sunlight filtering through the gritty windows. "So what. It got you to lighten up, didn't it?"

"Are we driving it to Grady's?" I opt for a neutral voice.

He slips his keys out of his pocket and tosses them to me. "Yeah, go ahead. It's all yours."

I swiftly shake my head and throw the keys back at him, like they're scorching hot. "No thanks. I don't want to."

He cocks an eyebrow, looking sexy. "What do you mean you don't want to?"

"I mean I don't want to drive it." It nearly kills me to say it. I walk around the front of the car, open the door, and gesture for Lila to get in.

"But it has a blown 572 Big Block in it," he says astounded with the keys hanging loosely from his fingers. "How can you not want to drive it?"

My insides twitch to drive it, but I won't buckle. "It's fine, Micha. I'd rather be the passenger."

"What does that mean? A blown big block or whatever you said?" Lila wonders as she walks to the side of the car. "Wait, are you guys talking cars? El doesn't like cars. In fact, she made us take the bus most of the time when we left campus."

"Oh really?" His tone implies otherwise. "That's news to me."

"It's a waste of gas," I lie, attempting to mask the truth; that I miss it. The rush, the speed, the adrenaline high.

Lila ducks inside the car and into the backseat. I climb into the passenger side and Micha opens the garage door. He revs up the engine, letting it rumble, teasing me, before backing down the driveway.

"I'm starting to think that the Ella you knew isn't the same one as I know." Lila buckles her seatbelt up.

He spins the tires down the road. "I think you might be on to something Lila, because the one I knew loved cars. In fact she used to hang out in the garage all day with the guys while the other girls played with their hair and makeup." He flashes me a dangerous grin. "She used to get all *excited* when we'd go racing."

No matter how hard I try to hinder myself from getting energized, I can't. Those hot summer nights, flying down the highway, neck and neck with another car, the rush soaring through my body.

Micha trails his finger along my neck and rests it on my pulse. "You're getting excited just thinking about it."

His touch spreads a longing through my body. I swat his hand away, cross my arms, and focus on the window, watching the neighborhood blur by as he cruises over the speed limit. Micha shifts the gears and the engine thunders louder, begging to burn rubber.

"Is it legal to be driving this fast?" Lila asks nervously. We glance back at her and she grips the edge of the leather seat. "It just seems like we're going really fast, especially in a neighborhood."

Micha holds my gaze resolutely as he downshifts and pumps up the rpms. "What do you think? Speed up? Or slow down?"

I want to tell him to slow down, pull on my seatbelt, and look away, but a passion that was dead raves. He throttles the gas pedal, keeping his eyes on mine, venturing me to look away first.

"Um… I don't think this is a good idea." Lila's voice is far away.

The car surges faster down the narrow road and his eyes dare me to tell him to slow down and part of me wants to. *Desperately.* But as he shoves the shifter into the next gear, going faster and faster, my body pleads to let go.

Suddenly, Lila screams, "Stop sign!"

Micha's eyes sparkle like sunlight reflecting into the ocean. He slams on the brakes, squealing the car to a halt, and throwing us all forward. My hand shoots out and I brace myself from hitting the dashboard.

"Are you crazy?" Lila's voice cracks as she situates back into the seat and realigns her dress over her legs. "What is wrong with you two?"

Micha and I look at each other and my body is burning with a hidden desire that I won't admit exists. My heart beats in my chest, rock steady and alive again. For a second, I'm back in the place I lost.

Then Micha ruins it.

"See, the same old Ella still lives." He grins arrogantly as he drives through the intersection. "She just needed a little push out."

I click the seatbelt locked, proving a point. "No, she doesn't. She's gone forever."

"Try all you want, but I'm bringing her back." He bites his lip, refocusing on the street as he mutters, "I won't let that night ruin you forever."

But it did. It broke me into a million pieces and blew them away in the wind, like crumbled leaves. That night was one of the most incredible nights I've ever had.

Then I quickly plummeted toward rock bottom.

Chapter 5

Micha

There she is, the girl I used to know. It's visible in her green eyes that she's getting turned on. She was always weird like that, the speed, the danger always got her own engine burning. Then I have to slow down and all the fire dissolves. She puts on her seatbelt and mutters something about the Ella I know being gone forever, but I'm calling her out. I have big plans to bring my best friend back, whether she likes it or not.

She's wearing a short skirt and tank top that's tight enough to show off her curves. It's driving me crazy that I can't touch her.

"What happened to the turnout?" she asks as we drive by the spot we use to park at during small town cruising. "It looks like you can't even take the road up to the cove anymore."

"You can if you walk or have four-wheel drive and ramp the hill." The turnout is blocked off by a large fence so that no cars can reach the dirt road that leads to a secluded area near the lake. "They blocked it off after they busted a bunch of people for drug and alcohol possession."

"Anyone I know?" she inquires, feigning indifference.

I thrum my fingers on top of the steering wheel. "Yeah, you're sitting next to one of them. But mine was only for alcohol."

Her friend gasps in the backseat and I catch Ella secretly rolling her eyes.

"What'd you get?" she asks nonchalantly.

"Probation and anger management classes." I return her indifference.

Her head turns toward me. "Anger management classes?"

"I also punched Grantford Davis in the face," I explain. "Pretty hard. Broke his nose and everything."

Her friend gasps again and I wonder how Ella could be friends with her. She seems like a naïve princess.

Ella studies me acutely with her beautiful eyes that always give away what she's really thinking. "Why did you punch him?"

"I think you know why." I carry her gaze forcefully.

"I asked him to drive me to the bridge, Micha," she says it like it strangles her. "It wasn't his fault. He was just doing it as a favor."

"He should have never left you there alone." I flip the blinker on, making a turn down a dirt road that leads into a field of tall, dry grass. "Not in that condition. You could barely think straight. In fact, do you even remember anything about that night?"

She fiddles with a band of bracelets on her wrists. "I'm not sure."

"Are you not sure?" I accuse. "Or do you not want to admit it?"

She starts to open her mouth, but then clamps her lips shut, and turns toward the window, dismissing me and the conversation.

Ella

The night I went to the bridge, I had been in a weird funk the entire day. My mom died a few weeks earlier and I couldn't seem to get rid of this vile feeling in my chest and I wanted it to go away. *Badly.* So I took drastic measures and decided to walk in my mother's footsteps for a night.

My mom wasn't awful. She had her good moments, but had a lot of bad ones too. When she was up, she was great—a lot of fun. At least that's what I thought when I was young. However, when I got older, there was a painful realization that it wasn't normal to go on huge shopping sprees, take off in the middle of the night for a road trip, pretend she could fly…

But the night on the bridge wasn't the worst night I'd ever experienced. It was just the last push to my rapid decline toward the loss of control over my life.

"Ella, where are you?" Micha's voice snaps me out of my own head. "You were dazing off on me there."

We're parked in front of Grady's single-wide trailer located in a field, near a junkyard and an abandoned apartment complex. I unbuckle my seatbelt, climb out of the car, and flip the seat forward to let Lila out.

"No thanks." She shakes her head, cowering back in the seat. "I think I'll wait in here."

"You're much safer inside." Micha points to a crumbling shack in the middle of the field. "That's a crack house over there and trust me, if they see you sitting in here, by yourself, they're going to come over and harass you."

Micha's messing with her, but I let him be because this place isn't that safe of a spot.

Her face pinches and she scrambles out of the car. "Who is this person's house we're at? It's not a drug dealer, is it?"

"No, it's just an old friend." I trade a secret glance with Micha and feelings rush through me like the sun and the wind. Grady was once Micha's stepfather. His mother and Grady were married for a few years and most of our happy childhood memories consist of him, camping, fishing, working on cars. Between the ages of eight and nine life was solid, not broken to pieces.

I meet Micha around the front of the car and when he takes my hand, I don't object. Being here is like traveling through time and it hurts to know that the man who showed me that life can be good is dying.

Lila tugs the bottom of her dress down self-consciously. "Are you sure I'm okay going in here?"

"Relax," I tell her as we reach the rickety front porch. "Grady is a good guy, he just likes living an unmaterialistic lifestyle. He chooses to live in a place like this."

She forces a tense smile. "Alright, I'm relaxing."

Micha squeezes my hand and then knocks on the door. A few knocks later and we let ourselves in. It's like I remember, and it makes me smile because it's comforting. Grady was a big traveler when he was younger and his walls map his destinations; petite nesting dolls from his trip to Russia on a small bookshelf, a painted Bokota mask from Africa hooked to the wall, a large hookah from Nepal sitting on a small fold up table. It overwhelms me and tugs at my memories.

The trailer is small with a narrow kitchen connected to a boxed in living room and the three of us nearly fill up the space.

Micha slides his hand up my arm and draws me to him. "Are you going to be okay?"

I nod, forcing the tears away. Micha kisses my temple and I don't retreat this time, allowing myself one small moment.

"It'll be okay," Micha says. "And I'm here for you."

Time's up.

"Where is he?" I take a deep breath, move away from Micha, and smother the old Ella away. He points over my shoulder. I turn around and my heart drops to my stomach. The medium build, tall man, with bright blue eyes and a head full of hair, has shifted into a frail, skeletal figure, with sunken eyes and his head shaved. His plaid jacket drowns his body and the belt around his jeans has holes added to it.

I hesitate to hug him. "How are you? Are you okay?"

"I'm always okay. You know that. Not even a little cancer can bring me down." He smiles and it's just as bright as it was. Using his cane, he hobbles toward me. I meet him halfway, in front of the tattered leather recliner and give him a gentle hug, afraid I might break him.

"How have you been, my little Ella May?" He steps back to take a look at me. "You look different."

I self-consciously touch my hair. "I changed my looks a little. Thought I could use a change or two."

He shakes his head contemplatively. "No, it's not that. There's something else. You seem sad."

"I'm fine," I deny and not very well. "I feel great."

He offers me a tolerant smile. "You've never been a good liar, you know that. I always knew it was you who broke the vase."

From behind me, Micha nods concurring. "It's her eyes. They show way too much. Although she thinks differently."

"If you knew I broke the vase," I say, "then why didn't you call me out on it?"

Grady laughs and exchanges a look with Micha. "Because the elaborate story you made up won my heart over, I guess. Besides, it was just a vase."

The tension resolves, except with Lila who looks like she doesn't know what to do with herself. She dawdles near the door, fidgeting with her watch and her hair as she glances around the snug trailer.

"Grady, this is Lila," I introduce, motioning her to come closer. "She was my college roommate."

Lila steps forward and gives him a small wave. "It's nice to meet you."

"Same here." Grady nods his head welcomingly and then arches his eyebrows at me. "So college? That's where you ran off to."

"I'm sorry I didn't tell you when I called," I apologize. "I just needed a break. From everything."

"I'm not going to lie and say it didn't hurt a little." He rests his weight on the cane, and his arms and legs look too thin to be moving. "You're like a daughter to me and I thought you trusted me enough to come to me if you were going through something."

His eyes dart to Micha and I wonder if he's told Grady about that night eight months ago on the bridge.

"I need to make a phone call." Micha holds up his phone as he backs for the door. "Lila, why don't you come outside with me?"

Lila gladly obliges and the door swings shut behind them, rocking the house.

Grady collapses into the recliner, sighing with relief. "We need to talk."

Preparing myself for a lecture, I drop into the con-caved sofa across from him. "I'm in trouble, aren't I?"

"Do you think you need to be in trouble?" He props his cane against the coffee table.

I pull a throw pillow on my lap and slump back into the couch. "I don't know. It's hard to tell what's right and what's wrong anymore or what's up and what's down even."

He rocks in the recliner. "You've always had a good grasp on what's right and wrong. You just have a hard time admitting that sometimes you choose the wrong."

"I know that." I gesture at myself. "That's why I changed into an Ella who doesn't do any wrong and who can keep control of her life."

"That's not what this is. This is you running from life and you can't control everything. Even if you want to." His words send a chill through my spine.

I pluck at a loose thread on the pillow. "Did Micha tell you about the night before I left... did he tell you what happened—what I did?"

He presses his cracked lips together. "He did."

"So then you understand why I ran away. If I don't change, then I'll turn out like her—I'll turn out just like my mother," I admit aloud for the first time and a weight lifts from my chest, but falls right back on it, seeming ten times heavier. "I'll lose control."

He hunches forward with a sad expression on his exhausted face. "You know I knew your mother really well."

"But only because you always had to come fix everything after she had one of her episodes."

"Sweetie, you're not her. Your mother was sick—she had a mental illness."

"Bipolar Disorder is hereditary," I say quietly. "There's a higher chance that I have it just because she had it."

"But it doesn't mean you will." With unsteady legs, he pushes up from the chair and sits down next to me on the sofa. "I think you're so afraid that you'll end up like your mom that you're hiding who you really are, but you can't control everything—no one can."

"But I can try," I mutter and sit up, tossing the pillow off my lap. "You remember what I was like. All the crap I did. The stupid, irresponsible crap. I was a wreck waiting to happen and that night proved it. I almost... I... I almost killed myself."

"No, you didn't. I heard the story and you would have never gone through with it," he says confidently. "You were just trying to sort through some stuff. You still are."

"No, I was going to do it," I tell him, but it's a lie. "My mind may have been hindered, but I remember enough to know that when I climbed on top of that bridge, I was going to jump."

He shakes his head. "Then you don't remember what happened afterward with Micha."

"Yeah, I do." I take a faltering breath. "I kissed him and then left him on the bridge. Then I went home, packed up my stuff, and ran away."

82

"No, something else happened that night." His forehead scrunches. "Micha took you somewhere else. At least that's what he told me."

I scratch at my wrist, trying to recollect, but the events of that day are hazy. "I don't remember this at all."

"From what I understand you were out of it and pretty upset. Those two are not a good combination. Trust me, I've been there." His fingers seek his cane. "Micha saved you from jumping, but there's more to it than that."

"When you say you've been there, what do you mean exactly?"

"I mean, I've been at the place where it seems like the only way left is down."

I sift through his words. "You know, I came here to see if you're okay, and somehow all we've talked about is me."

"And that's exactly what I need," he says. "I'm sick and tired of everyone wanting to talk about my death."

I open my mouth, but the front door squeaks open. I expect Micha, but a middle-aged woman in black sweat pants and a white t-shirt walks in. Her bleached hair is woven into a braid and she's carrying a large black bag.

She grins at Grady as she shuts the door. "You're being bad again. You know you're not supposed to get out of bed."

Grady rolls his eyes, but his face lights up. "Yep, I've been bad. I guess you'll have to punish me."

I try to ignore their disturbing comments the best that I can, but it's ridiculously awkward.

"Ella, this is Amy." His serious demeanor alleviates as he says her name.

I stand up from the couch to shake hands with Amy, noticing there's no ring on her finger. "Are you his nurse?"

Grady starts to balance to his feet and she moves to help him, but he waves her off. "I got this. I'm not crippled yet. "

She sighs and moves back. "Yes, I'm his nurse and I'm supposed to be taking care of him, but he's a stubborn man and refuses to let me do my job properly."

He growls and then chuckles. Using his cane, he heads toward the hall, his feet dragging along the orange shaggy carpet. "Ella, can you stop by tomorrow? I want to talk to you some more."

"Okay, I'll come back," I promise as he vanishes down the hall. I turn to the nurse. "How bad is he?"

She drops the bag on the counter and unzips it. "What did he tell you?"

"That he has cancer," I tell her as she takes out some baggies from the bag. "But that's all. He doesn't like to open up about himself."

Reaching into her bag, she extracts a handful of pre-scription bottles. "No, he doesn't, does he?" She shakes a bottle filled with clear liquid. "He has stage four bone cancer."

I nearly fall to the floor. "Stage four, but then that means that…"

"It means that he has a hard, short road ahead of him," she says frankly. "You're Ella Daniels, right? And your father is Raymond Daniels?"

My fingers grasp the fabric of the recliner like it's a lifeline. "Yeah, why?"

"No reason," she says with a shrug. "Grady just talks about you sometimes."

"But you know my father," I state warily.

She zips up her bag and shuffles to the kitchen sink with the medication. "I was the nurse on call the night he was run over."

Because he was drunk out of his mind and decided to ride his bike in the middle of the highway. "So you take care of Grady, here at his home?"

She turns on the faucet and fills up a glass of water. "I'm the home nurse he hired after he decided he didn't want to spend his last months in a hospital bed."

He only has *months* left? I need to regain control of the spiraling situation. I stumble for the door. "Tell Grady I'll see him tomorrow."

I trip down the steps and nearly eat dirt. Luckily Micha is at the bottom and he drops his phone to catch me.

He steadies me to my feet, his fingers digging into my hips as he looks me over with concern. "Okay, what happened?"

"He's dying," I whisper, staring out at the dry field. "He's really dying."

"I know." Micha holds onto me forcefully, the tips of his fingers touching my bare skin. "I told you this before we came over here."

My lungs restrict oxygen. "I thought when you said it… well, I don't know what I thought, but not this." I wave my hand at the door without looking at it. "Not a nurse. Not a few months left."

His hands move around to my back and he enfolds me against his chest. I rest my head against him, breathing in his comforting scent. I start to ask him what happened that night, but my fear of the truth shushes me. What if it's bad? What if it pushes me over the edge?

"What do you want to do today?" he whispers. "You name it and it's done."

I pull away, blinking back the tears. My gaze travels to Lila sitting in the car, reapplying her lip gloss in the rear-view mirror. "I have to take her to the shop and get her on the road."

Against my protest, Micha cups the back of my head, and lures me against him. "You could just ditch her."

I slap his arm. "Since when are you mean to girls?"

"Since they keep complaining about the sheer drabness of the town," he says in a mocking cheerleader voice. "And the bugs. It's ridiculous. Ten minutes out here with her and I want to lead her into the crack house over there and run."

"That's not a crack house and you know it." I shake my head, forcing back a grin. "And I know you better than that. I'm sure you want to get in her pants."

He pauses, and then slowly his hand explores my back and sneaks to my ass. He grabs it, and bows my body into his, firing a heat deep inside my core and fumbling a moan from my lips. For a second, I forget where I am.

"The only thing I want to get in is you," he murmurs in my hair.

I regain control and shove back. "*Seriously*? You're going to start this? Here of all places."

He swings a hand at the trailer. "Why not? Because of Grady? He'd be happy to finally see us together. He's been saying for years that you and I will end up together."

I cover my ears. "I can't listen to this."

In three long strides, he's in my face, nearly stepping on my toes. "You think that just because you left, it would change how I feel? Well, guess what? You're wrong. I can't help how I feel. I'm still in—"

"Don't say it." I point a finger at him. "Don't you dare, Micha Scott."

He holds up his hands, wide-eyed and derisive. "Oh, now I'm in trouble. You used my last name and everything."

I glance at the car, checking if Lila's eavesdropping, then whirl back and hiss, "You are in trouble. I've been back for less than a day and everything I've worked on concealing is falling apart because of you."

His aqua eyes are a fierce blue. "Good. You're fucking crazy if you think that you can run off and change your identity. This unfeeling, preppy girl thing you got going on," he motions his hand at my tank top, white frilly skirt, and curly hair, "is nothing but bull shit. You can't just change who you are on the outside and expect it to change who you are on the inside."

Anger bubbles through me and I shove him. "You're wrong."

His boots scuff the dirt as he catches his balance and smiles haughtily. "Am I? Because right now that fire I love so much is burning pretty bright." He reaches for my cheek, to touch me— entice me.

"Micha, this is who I have to be otherwise I can't breathe. Please just leave it alone. That damn fire might exist, but I want it gone." I spin my back to him, praying he'll listen to me for once, because if he keeps it up, sooner or later I won't be able to resist.

But Micha has never backed down on a challenge in his life.

Chapter 6

Micha

The pain in her eyes nearly kills me. If it were possible, I'd
go back in time and stop her from climbing down that tree
that God awful night. Maybe then, I'd still have my best
friend.

I decide to make a sporadic stop to try and get Ella out
of her own head. I park the car in an open space in front of
the small coffeehouse located in the heart of town, between
the Stop n' Shop and Bubba's Sports Barn. I shut off the
engine and wait patiently for her to scold me.

Her face reddens as she takes in where we are.
"Micha, I'm really not in the mood for this right now. I
have things to do and so does Lila."

"Come on, you haven't seen me play in ages," I coax,
using my best seductive voice. "I'll just do one song. In
and out and we're done."

"Sounds cool to me," Lila says from the backseat, finally relaxing a little now that we're far away from Grady's trailer. "I love hearing bands and lead singers are always sexy."

"Micha plays the guitar and sings by himself," Ella says with a flicker of possessiveness in her eyes. "He's not a lead singer. He's a solo singer."

"It's all the same to me." Lila pats Ella's head and in a way I think she's making a private joke with her. "Band or not, a guy who can sing and play is hot."

I grin charismatically and incline over the console. "Come on, pretty girl." I wind a strand of her hair around my finger. "You know you want to come in and watch me be all hot and sexy, singing up on the stage. You know you've missed it."

Her eyes narrow at me as she fights back a smile. "You know that voice doesn't work on me. I've seen you use it too many times on too many girls."

"I haven't used it on a girl since you left." I let the truth fall out. I used to come and go as I please with whoever I wanted, but once things started to change with our friendship, it became clear the void I was trying to fill was in her. "And I don't want to use it on anyone—"

She conceals her hand over my mouth. "I'll go in with you, but only if you stop talking about stuff that makes me uncomfortable."

"Wait. What about my car?" Lila scoots forward and fixes her hair using the rearview mirror. "It's getting late. Won't the shop be closed soon?"

I move Ella's hand away from my lips and entwine her fingers with mine. "We'll make it back in time. I promise."

Ella hesitates, staring at the coffeehouse like she's a mouse about to walk into a lion's den.

I squeeze her hand. "Come on, let's go in. You'll be okay."

She looks at our hands, and then her gaze lifts, giving a fleeting glance at my lips before resolving on my eyes. "Is everyone still hanging out here?"

"Kelly and Mike do and Renee and Ethan," I say. "Grantford doesn't really come around here anymore, though."

Her plump lips curl to a grin. "Because you punched him in the face."

"That might be part of it." I return her smile and let go of her hand to climb out of the car. It feels like I might be getting somewhere with her.

She hops out and stretches, arching her back and sticking out her chest. It makes me want to rip off her shirt, pull her in the backseat, and do things to her I've never done with anyone I've cared about before.

"What are you looking at?" She pulls the bottom of her tank top back over her stomach.

She really has no idea how beautiful she is. She never has. Even back in her punk/goth faze, she rocked the look.

I shake my head, unable to take my eyes off her. "Nothing. Just thinkin'."

She slams the door and we head across the packed parking lot. I rest my hand on her lower back, but she wiggles away and sidesteps around Lila, putting her between us.

I frown. Maybe I'm not doing as well as I thought.

Ella

If he keeps looking at me that way, my restraint is going to melt into a puddle of hot, steamy liquid. Micha has the most piercing eyes in the world, aqua blue, like the sea, waved with equal intensity. He's flirty with me, which he used to do jokingly all the time, and I'd play along.

But this is different somehow, more intense and real. It's like he's throwing his heart into the open, which isn't how he used to be. At least with me. Except for the day I left.

The coffeehouse is cramped with people, even for a Saturday afternoon. Every booth and table is occupied and there's a guy with floppy brown hair playing the keyboard on stage, his voice a little off-key. The baristas are working hard on the long line that extends all the way to the door and in the corner, people are working on their laptops.

"Where are we going to sit?" Lila scans the room. "There's no empty tables."

Micha spots Ethan and Renee at a corner table and waves at them. "Seat situation solved," he says, taking my hand and leading the way to them.

Renee is a short girl that wears heavy eyeliner and has dark red hair. Her hazel eyes zone in on Micha's hand tangled with mine. I attempt to pull my hand away, but Micha strengthens his grasp.

"Hey, Ella." She fakes a smile with her dark red lips. "What ya been up to?"

"Nothing much," I keep it simple, because simple is always better with Renee.

"And so we meet again." Ethan flashes a dimpled grin at Lila and pulls out a chair for her. "You decided to stick around here for a while."

Lila looks up at him as she takes a seat. "Thank you. I kind of had to since my car was trashed last night."

Micha drops down in the last empty chair at the table and starts to pull me down to sit on his lap. My eyes sweep the room in search of an extra chair, but it's so packed that people have to stand near the walls.

"I don't bite, Ella May." There is a challenge in Micha's eyes. "Unless you ask me to."

Everyone at the table is watching me. Not wanting to make a scene, I sink down on his lap. Ethan targets Micha with a bewildered look, which Micha ignores and steals a scone out of a basket in the middle of the table.

He pops it into his mouth. "So what time's Open Mic?"

Ethan's dark eyebrows plunge together. "Why? Are you thinking about playing again? Cause' all I can say is it's about freakin' time."

"What do you mean again?" I ask, grabbing a scone myself. "Why hasn't he been playing?"

Ethan shoves up the sleeves of his shirt, crosses his arms on the table, and directs Micha with their secret-code look I have never been able to crack. I revolve my body to look at Micha, but instantly regret it. His eyes are too intense and I'm thrown out of my element for a second.

"You stopped playing?" I ask him. "Why would you do that? Isn't it your dream still?"

He shrugs, snaking his arms around my waist. "It's not the same without you here watching me."

"There were times I didn't watch you play." I put my hands on his shoulders. "Even when I lived here."

He shakes his head and wisps of his blonde hair fall across his forehead. "That's not true. You never missed one."

I think back, knowing he's right. "I don't want you to stop living your life because I'm not here anymore."

"And I don't want you to be anywhere but here." He squeezes my hip and I instinctively jump at the tingling heat that spirals down between my legs.

"What can I get you?" The waitress interrupts us. We all read off what we want, and the waitress gets particularly giggly when she writes down Micha's order, even though I'm sitting on his lap.

Her name is Kenzie and I've never liked her. She used to help Stacy Harris torment this girl we went to school with, who was in a wheelchair. I casually lean back against Micha's chest, as if I'm doing it by accident. No one seems to notice except for the waitress. And Micha. His heart beat speeds up as if the nearness of my body is driving him mad.

She frowns and tucks the order book into her apron. "I'll be right back with your drinks."

I wait for Micha to call me out, but he stays quiet and keeps his hands on the tops of my bare thighs. I know it's wrong and that he's not mine. I made that clear the day I bailed, but I can't seem to help myself. Ever since we were kids, I always felt the need to keep him away from girls who aren't good enough for him.

Old habits die hard.

Micha

Ethan is looking at me like I'm an idiot. Probably because I'm smiling like an idiot, but I can't help myself. Ella got territorial with the waitress. She's never done that before, not even before she left.

"This band's interesting," Lila hollers over the banjo band playing up on stage. "Is this the kind of music you play?"

Ethan, Renee, and I burst out laughing. Even Ella covers her mouth, trying really hard not to laugh.

"No sweetie, this isn't what I play." I gulp my coffee. "Mines more…"

"Hot and sexy," Ella says and I stare at her. She ignores my gaze and adds, "Think more along the lines of Spill Canvas."

Lila brushes some crumbs off the table. "That band you're always listening to when you're studying?"

Ella nods, but shifts awkwardly. "That's the one."

It makes me feel better that she still listens to the same music. At least that hasn't changed. I keep one hand on her leg, afraid if I release her completely, she'll run off again. I steal another scone from the basket and pop it into my mouth. Lila starts chatting with Ethan and Renee gets on her cellphone.

I sweep Ella's hair to the side and put my lips to her ear. "So you think I'm hot and sexy, huh?"

She bites back a smile, pretending to be deeply immersed in the banjo song. "No, I said your music is hot and sexy."

"It's all the same." I dare a kiss against her shoulder, relishing the softness of her skin, wanting her so God damn bad I'm getting a hard on just thinking about it.

Ella notices it too and squirms around in my lap, making it worse. "Down boy," she jokes with a nervous laugh, then presses her lips together and starts to stand up.

I trap her down by the hips and conform her backside onto my lap. We fit together so perfectly it's mind blowing and all those feelings I felt for her before she left come rushing back to me. I need more of her. *Now*. Oblivious to everyone around us, my hands gradually slide up her thighs.

"Micha." She protests with a quiver in her voice. "Don't. There are people…"

I silence her as my fingers brush the edges of her skirt. I can't stop—I've been carrying this sexual tension for ages. I started having these feelings for her when we were

98

about sixteen. I ignored them for as long as possible, because I knew she'd freak if she found out. There were a few stolen kisses that I played off, but the night on the bridge, when I finally put it out there, changed everything. She freaked out just like I thought.

Right after she left, I slept around, trying to get rid of the hunger inside of me, but after a while, I realized there was no point. Ella had taken something from me and there was no getting it back, unless I had her.

So I let my hands sneak up the edge of her skirt and her fingers knead into my thighs. I wonder how far I should take this, since we're sitting in a booth in a crowded room, and I almost pull back, but one of her legs falls to the side, and I view it as an open invitation.

"Alright, it's time for open mic." The waitress that undressed me with her eyes speaks into the microphone on the stage. "If you already haven't signed up, you can sign up with Phil over there." She points her finger at the owner, a middle-aged man sitting in the corner next to the speakers.

"I think that's your cue." Ella quickly gets up, thinking she's off the hook.

Before I head up to the signup sheet, I spread my fingers across her lower back and whisper in her ear, "Don't think this is over because it's not."

She shivers and I strut off to the table with a satisfied smile on my face.

"Well, son of a bitch," Phil says from behind the table. He's an ex-band member of an 80's cover band and still looks like he belongs in that decade with his mullet and neon clothes. "Look what the dog dragged in."

"Miss me that bad, huh?" I jot down my name on the signup sheet.

"Are you kidding me?" he asks. "All we've had to listen to for the last few months is banjo music and a couple of hippies playing on the bongos. I swear it's like Woodstock all over again."

I laugh, dropping the pen onto the table. "Well it's nice to know I've been missed, I guess."

Phil fiddles with the volume of the amps. "More than missed. Please tell me you're going to start playing here again. I'm in desperate need of some draw-in. This place is going downhill."

I smile politely, backing toward the table. "Nah, probably not. I don't think I'm going to be sticking around here much longer. I've got places to go, people to see."

On my way back to the table, I cross paths with Naomi. She is Phil's daughter, tall, with long black hair, and she's an awesome singer. I used to play with her back before she went on the road with a band. We were actually pretty close, but I haven't talked to her since she left.

"Oh my God, I'm so glad I ran into you," she says and there's a little bit of red lipstick on her teeth.

"Isn't everyone?" I tease walking backwards.

She laughs and swats my arm. "I see you still have that whole cocky attitude going."

I drop the act. "So you're back in town?"

"Yeah, but only for a few weeks. Can we chat up after you play? There's something I really need to talk to you about. Something huge actually."

"How'd you know I was playing?"

She points a finger at the table. "I just saw you sign up."

"Alright, I'll catch up with you later." I wave good-bye, wondering what she could possibly want.

Ella

Damn Micha. He's killing me with his touches and longing gazes and now he's going to sing. I've always had a soft spot for his voice. We'd sit on his bed and he'd strum his guitar while I sketched. Those were some of the perfect moments in my life.

"Ella, what's the matter with you?" Lila asks with an accusation. "You look a little flushed."

101

I sip my latte and realign the holder in the center of the table, so I can't see my reflection in the stainless steel. "It's just a little hot in here. That's all."

"Yeah, sure it is." She won't stop looking at me, like she's trying to crack open my head.

As Micha steps onto the stage not too far from our table, my heart starts to chant unspeakable words.

Sitting on a stool with his guitar on his lap he puts his lips up to the microphone, nibbling on his lip ring. "This one's called 'What No One Ever Sees'."

He strums a chord with his eyes locked on me,

"I see it in your beautiful eyes, like a spot on the sun.
The things you want to hide, buried deep inside you.
Blinded by your light.
It almost hurts to look at, almost hurts to breathe.
Never can you look at the things no one ever sees
Shaded by your light.
Please take me inside you, please take me in.
Never will I whisper, never will I give in.
Even when I'm dying, your heart will always win.
Shielded to the sightless, isolated from the naïve.
Breaking you in pieces, that can only ever grieve.
Veiled by your light.
Passionate for the world, yet overlooked by most.
Your soul flickers in you, desperate to shine for the world

But blinded by your darkness.
Please take me inside you, please take me in.
Never will I whisper, never will I give in.
Even when I'm dying, your heart will always win."

With one lasting note, he ends the song. The crowd applauds and my eyes dart away from his penetrating gaze, and to the door. I want to run away like the room is on fire.

"Holy crap," Lila breathes, fanning herself. "You were right. That was HOT."

"I can play the drums." Ethan taps his fingers on the table, and makes drum noises. "And I'm pretty good."

"Don't let him fool ya." Renee sips her coffee and a smirk curls at her lips. "He can play the drums on *Rock Band* and that's it."

Ethan shoots Renee a dirty look. "Would you quit it? It's not funny anymore."

Lila looks at me for an explanation.

"This is how they are," I explain with a heavy sigh. "They fight like cats and dogs."

Lila props her elbows onto the table and rests her chin on her hands. "El, doesn't your brother play drums?"

"Yeah, Dean did," I say. "A little bit, anyway."

"Now Dean's hot," Renee remarks, aiming to get under my skin.

Micha collects his guitar and clears the stage for the next singer, a girl with pink dreads who looks like she has a grudge against the world. A tall girl with long legs meets Micha at the corner of the stage. Her wavy black hair flows down her back, her grey eyes are striking, and her smile is bright. Her name is Naomi and she's the daughter of the owner of the coffeehouse, who Micha played with a few times.

She says something to Micha and he laughs. A flicker of envy burns in me, but I suppress it quickly. She leads him off the stage and Micha's hand roams toward her back. He flashes me one last glance, before he ducks behind stage. I can't read him at all and that frightens me more than when I can.

Lila drinks her soy latte and peeks at me over the brim of her cup. "I don't care what you say. That boy is in love with you."

I stay silent, tearing up a napkin until it's shaped like a heart. "He might be, but not the kind of love you're talking about."

"So, Ella," Ethan interrupts and I swear he does it intentionally. If he did, I'm thankful for it. "How's the city life?"

"Stupendous." I ruffle up the napkin and toss it into the empty scone basket.

"That doesn't sound very convincing." Ethan drapes an arm on the back of Lila's chair and places his foot on his knee. "Don't you like it there?"

I force myself to cheer up and sit up straight. "Actually, it's pretty nice. There's a lot to do and the school is great."

"You're acting weird." Ethan eyes me, rubbing his chin. "Something's got you all wound up."

"I'm completely okay," I say in denial. "Although, the excessive questions are a bit much."

Lila peers over at me as she licks froth from her lips. "He's right. You look upset or something." She feels my forehead. "You're not getting sick, are you?"

Micha returns to the table and the coffeehouse has cleared out a bit. He grabs a vacant chair, pulls it up to the table, turning it backwards, and then sits down in it.

"So what are we up to for the rest of the night?" Ethan asks while Micha checks his messages on his phone.

"I got to take this pretty lady over here to get her car fixed by you." Micha nods his head at Lila.

Ethan looks pleased. "Wow, I'm honored to be the one to fix it."

Micha slides his phone into his pocket. "We have to swing by Ella's house and pick it up, so meet us at the shop in like a half-an-hour."

"Absolutely." Ethan waves the waitress over to give us the check.

"What do you think?" Micha asks me. "Does it sound like a plan?"

I shrug, distracted by where he went with that girl. "Yeah, sure."

Everyone takes their coffee's to-go and we head for the door. I leave mine behind, along with something else, but I'm not sure what.

Perhaps a piece of my new identity.

***

Micha and I don't speak the entire drive home. It freaks Lila out a little and I worry that the more time she spends here with me, the less time she's going to want to spend with me on campus. When we pull into the driveway that routes the side of my house, there is a painful reminder of another reason I didn't want to come back waiting for me near the garage.

"Whose car is *that*?" Lila scoots forward in her seat. "It's gorgeous."

"Why is he here?" I grimace, scowling at the shiny red Porsche with Ohio license plates.

"Now be nice," Micha warns, his voice dripping with sarcasm. "He's your brother."

"But it doesn't make him less of an asshole," I mutter. "And he swore when he left, he was never coming back here ever again."

"That's your brother's car?" Lila asks. "Good God, what does he do for living?"

I press the tips of my fingers to the sides of my nose. "Who knows?"

"Well, how does he afford a car like that?" she requests interestedly.

"It's not his car," I say. "It's my mothers."

Micha and I swap an oblique look, recalling the day the car mysteriously showed up in the garage. She never would tell anyone how she got it, and for a while, Dean and I expected the police to show up and arrest her for car thievery. It never happened and as time went on, it became like a game to my mother. Not just with the car, but with life. We never knew if she was telling the truth or not.

After she died, Dean took the car. He acted like it was his right and maybe it was. He wasn't the one who'd snuck out of the house that night and left our mother alone.

"And that gorgeous car over there is yours," I remind Lila, diverting her attention elsewhere. "You should probably go get it fixed, before Ethan wanders off from the shop."

She slumps back in the chair. "I'd really like to meet your brother first before I go."

"I'm sure he'll still be here when you get back." Actually I'm hoping he'll be gone.

"Come on, Lila, we'll make it quick." Micha opens the door. "We can drop it off and walk back. It isn't too far."

When I climb outside, he captures my gaze over the roof of the car. "Are you coming with us?"

"I think I need to stay." My eyes travel to the back door. "Who knows why he's here and what he'll say to dad? And I don't think dad can handle his crap."

Pressing his hands to the roof, he leans over. "But can you handle his crap?"

"I'll be fine," I assure him. "Just get her car fixed. She needs to get out before she gets sucked into this place."

"This town isn't that bad." Micha closes the door. "You used to think the same thing."

"I also used to believe my mom would get better," I say. "And look what a crashing disappointment that was."

From the back of the car, Lila blinks at me, stunned. "Ella, I didn't know your mom was sick."

Micha's expression is guarded. "Let's go, Lila. Ella's right, if Ethan gets too bored, he'll bail."

They head for Lila's car and I head up the driveway, wishing I could run back into Micha's arms and alleviate the hole in my chest.

Micha

I worry about Ella the entire drive to the shop. Dean was never a good brother and at the funeral, he blamed Ella for their mother's death. He basically tore her to shreds. Maybe it was his way of mourning, but it was still a shitty thing to do.

"So what's up with Ella and her brother?" Lila asks, resting her arm on the console.

"I think that's something you should probably talk to her about." I turn the car into the parking lot of the shop. "It's not really my story to tell."

Lila unclips her seatbelt. "But Ella's never really told me much about her life. She has always been so quiet about it and I just thought it was her personality, but the way everyone talks about her around here, I don't think it is."

"She used to be pretty loud spoken." I reach for the door, but hesitate, needing to get it off my chest. "The Ella I knew was not the prim and proper girl you've been hanging out with. She had this fire in her and she didn't put up with anyone's crap. It got her into trouble a lot, but she was also the kind of person who would take the fall, even if it wasn't her fault."

"I think I saw that part of her when we stopped at a bathroom when we first got to town," Lila muses. "There was this guy there who was giving me crap and Ella nearly beat him up."

I try not to smile. "She did, did she?"

"Is that how she was when you knew her? Like a total badass?" Lila grins and I realize she's not as bad as I originally thought.

"Yeah, she was always kind of a badass." I shove the door open and my boots scuff the gravel as I climb out.

There are a few cars parked in front of the metal building and both the garage doors are open. A truck is parked inside and the owner of the shop—Ethan's dad—is working under the hood.

"So what do you do?" Lila asks as we head to the entrance.

"A little of this," I joke. "And a little of that."

"So it's a secret." She picks up on my vibe.

I swing the chain attached to my jeans. "For now, it kind of is."

"Gotcha." She doesn't press and I like her even more.

Ethan is waiting for us in the lobby, slouched back in a chair with his shoes kicked up on the counter and his head slanted back. "It's about damn time. I was about ready to leave."

Lila starts to giggle as she takes out her phone from her purse. "You guys weren't lying."

Ethan lowers his feet to the floor and stands up. "What's so funny?"

"Nothing." I shrug him off, resting my arms on the counter. "Ella and I just told her that if we didn't hurry up you'd get bored and leave."

"So you were talking about me behind my back." He walks around the counter by Lila. "You got the keys or did you leave them in?" I toss him the keys and he catches them. "Where's Ella?"

"Her brother showed up," I explain. "She's back at her house."

Ethan's eyebrows shoot upward. "And you left her there alone with him?"

"Only to drop this off," I say. "Lila and I are going to walk back."

Lila glances back and forth between Ethan and me. "Is something wrong with Ella's brother?"

"She'll be fine." I lean against the glass door with my arms folded and check my watch. "But we should get back."

"I think I should stay here," Lila says, frowning at her phone.

"Are you sure?" I ask. "Ethan will take good care of it."

She looks upset as she tosses the phone into her purse. "Yeah, I need to make sure everything's taken care of properly."

"Alright, can you find your way back to the house?" I nudge the door open.

"I'll make sure she gets there," Ethan offers with a shrug.

Lila adjusts her purse on her shoulder and gives him a small smile. "Thank you."

"Alright, if it's okay with the both of you, then I guess I'll see you later." I hike across the parking lot, toward the street. It's getting late, and the odds of Lila's car being fixed by the end of the day are pretty fucking low. I take out my cell phone and text Ella.

Me: Just wantin to make sure ur ok?

I walk down the sidewalk fenced by houses and dried out lawns. There is a drug exchange going on at the corner between a group of kids that still look young enough to be in high school. This side of town is pretty crappy, which I'm okay with now, but when Ella and I were kids, it was harder to deal with.

Ella was always so curious about stuff. There were many times we got chased down for sticking our noses where they didn't belong and I got my ass kicked defending Ella quite a few times.

But I'd do it again in a heartbeat because when it all comes down to it, it's just me and her against the world. Always has been.

My phone buzzes inside my pocket and I check the message, surprised to see Ella's name on the screen.

Ella: No, I don't think I am.

Without a second thought, I run as fast as I can toward her house.

Chapter 7

Ella

Dean's got his music blasting upstairs at full volume and it's rattling the ceiling. I start picking up the garbage in the kitchen, avoiding the confrontation of seeing him again. Propping the trash can against my hip, I drag my arm along the counter, pushing a line of bottles into it.

I pull out the bag and tie the string shut, holding it far away from me. "God, that stinks."

"Still cleaning up after dad, I see." Dean enters the kitchen. He's dressed in slacks and a button down shirt, the sleeves rolled up to his elbows. His dark brown hair is cut short and it shows off the scar on the top of his forehead, where I accidently hit him during a freak accident while we were playing baseball with a tent pole and a basketball. "Nothing changes around here, even when you leave for a year." He opens the fridge and steals a beer.

"Although, you do look different. Did you finally clean up your act?"

"Do you really care if I did?" I drag the garbage bag toward the back door. "I think you made it perfectly clear the last time you were here that you don't give a shit what happens to me."

He pops the cap off the bottle. "Are you still on that?"

"You told me I killed our mother," I say quietly. "How could I be over that?"

He sips his beer and shrugs. "I thought you left so you could move on with your life."

I summon a deep breath. "I didn't move on. I bailed just like you did."

"I ran away for the same reason you ran away because staying here means dealing with the past and our pasts are the kind that need to be locked away and never revisited."

"You mean dealing with mom's death. And the fact that it was my fault she's dead. Or that I'm responsible for her death."

He peels at the beer bottle label. "Why do you always have to be so blunt about everything? It makes people uncomfortable."

I'm changing back into my old ways and I need to collect myself. Opening the back door, I toss the garbage bag onto the back steps. "Do you want to go get some dinner or something? We could go out to Alpine where no one really knows us."

He shakes his head, gulps down the rest of the beer, and then tosses the empty bottle into the trash. "The only reason I came back here was to get the rest of my stuff. Then I'm out. I got stuff to go back to that's more important than family drama and alcoholic fathers."

He leaves me in the kitchen and a few seconds later, the music is turned up louder. It's an upbeat rhythm and it drives me crazy, so I crank on the kitchen radio, blasting "Shameful Metaphors" by *Chevelle*.

I start sweeping up the kitchen, blocking out my brother's words. He always liked to nitpick me apart, which was fine, but at the funeral, he crossed a line we can never come back from.

The back door swings open and the wind rushes in as my dad stumbles into the kitchen. His shoes are untied, his jeans are torn, and his red shirt is stained with dirt and grease. His hand is wrapped with an old rag that's soaked in blood.

Dropping the broom to the floor, I rush to him. "Oh my God, are you okay?"

He flinches from me and nods his head, staggering to the sink. "Just cut myself on the job. No biggie."

I turn down the music. "Dad, you weren't drinking at work, were you?"

He turns the faucet on and his head slumps over. "The guys and I had a couple of shots during lunch break, but I'm not drunk." He removes the rag and sticks his hand under the water, letting out a relieved sigh as the water mixes with his blood. "Is your brother home? I thought I saw his car in the driveway."

I grab a paper towel and clean up the blood he got on the counter and on the floor. "He's upstairs packing up some stuff or something."

He dabs his hand with a paper towel, wincing. "Well, that's good I guess."

I lean over to examine his hand. "Do I need to take you to the doctor? That looks like it might need stitches?"

"I'll be fine." He grabs a bottle of vodka, takes a swig, and then douses his hand with it.

"Dad, what are you doing?" I reach for the first aid kit above the sink. "Use the rubbing alcohol from the first aid kit."

Breathing through clenched teeth, he wraps up his hand with a paper towel. "See, good as new."

"It can still get infected." I take out the kit and set it on the counter. "You should really let me take you to a doctor."

He stares at me for a moment with his eyes full of agony. "God, you look so much like her, it's just crazy... "He drags his feet as he walks out the doorway and into the

117

living room. Seconds later, I hear the television click on and the air fills with smoke.

Suppressed feelings surface as I put the first aid kit back into the cupboard. Cranking up the music, I drown out my pain and busy myself with the dishes. My phone vibrates in my pocket and I wipe my hands off on a towel before checking my messages. There's the voicemail from Micha from yesterday that I still haven't listened to and a new text message from him.

The text message seems like the less dangerous of the two. My hand trembles as I read it over and over again, then finally respond. I toss the phone on the counter and focus on cleaning because it's simple. And simple is just what I want.

Micha

I barge into Ella's house. Something bad happened, probably because of her douche bag brother. Ella is scrubbing down the counters with the same amount of energy as a drummer. Her hair is pulled up, but pieces hang loose in her face. She has the music on, so she doesn't hear me come in. I walk up behind her, wanting to touch her, but instead I turn the music down.

She drops the paper towel she is holding and reels around. "You scared the hell out of me." She presses her hand to her chest. "I didn't hear you come in."

"That's kind of obvious." I search her green eyes, crammed with misery.

She fidgets with a stack of plates and carries them over to the cupboard before backtracking to the sink. She's wound up over something and too much energy is in her. Her mom was like that a lot of times. But Ella's not her mother, whether she realizes it or not.

I collect the plates from her hand and set them in the sink. "Do you want to tell me what's got you all worked up?"

Tapping her fingers on the sides of her legs, she shakes her head. "I should have never sent you that text. I don't know why I did it."

She starts to turn away from me, but I catch the bottom of her shirt. "Ella May, stop talking to me like we're business associates. I know you better than anyone and I know when something's bothering you."

"I said I was fine." Her voice is tight as she forces back the tears. The girl never lets herself cry, even when her mom died.

"No, you're not." I steer her by the shoulders toward me. "And you need to let it out."

She stares at the floor. "I can't."

I tuck my finger under her chin and raise her head up, looking into her eyes. "Yes, you can. It's killing you inside."

Her shoulders quiver and she lets her head fall against my chest. I rub her back and tell her it will be okay. It's not much, but it's enough for the moment.

Finally she pulls back and her face is unreadable. "Where's Lila?"

"I left her with Ethan at the shop." I sit down on the kitchen table that's stacked with unopened bills. "She's supposed to come back here when her car's fixed."

She gazes out the window, lost in her thoughts. "She could just go home after Ethan's done. She doesn't need to come back here."

"Where does she live?"

"In California."

"Then she probably shouldn't leave tonight." I glance out the window at the sun setting behind the shallow hills. "It's late and she's going to be driving by herself, right?"

Ella nods, spaced out as she twists her hair around her finger. "And I worry about her making the drive by herself. I mean she practically freaked out when we ran into Grantford at the restrooms over by the lake."

My fingers grip the edge of the table. "You ran into *Grantford?*"

She lowers her hand from her hair and lets it fall to her side. "Yeah, but it wasn't a big deal. He just acted like himself and you know how that is."

I release the table from my death grip, trying to clear the anger out of my head. No matter what Ella says, Grantford never should have left her on the bridge that night when she was that out of it.

I stretch my legs out in front of me and change the direction of the conversation. "How *did* you end up becoming friends with Lila?"

She bites down on her lip, contemplating. "We were roommates." She shrugs, letting her lip pop out from her teeth and it drives me crazy because all I want to do is bite down on it myself. "She was really nice and different from all my friends here and I wanted a change."

I hop off the table and move in front of her. "Change is good, but completely shutting down is a whole other story, Ella, have you... Did you ever talk to anyone about what happened with your mom?"

Her shoulders stiffen and she turns for the doorway, preparing to leave. "That's none of your business."

I block her path. "Yes it is. I've known you forever, so I get full rights to what's inside your head."

Her eyes narrow and she puts her hands on her hips. "Get out of my way, Micha Scott."

"What is it with you using my last name?" I say. "Before, when you'd get mad at me, you'd just call me a douche bag."

"I don't use those words anymore," she says flatly. "I'm nicer than that."

"Really?" I accuse. "Because you sure seem pissed off at me all the time."

"I'm trying not to be," she fumes. "But you're making it very hard for me."

"Alright, you need a time out. I've had enough of your stubborn crap." I pick her up by the waist and throw her over my shoulder.

She lets out a startled gasp, and pounds her fists onto my back. "Dammit Micha, put me down!"

Ignoring her, I walk out the back door and down the empty driveway. I think about grabbing her ass just because I can, but I'm afraid she might bite me... although, that doesn't sound bad.

"Micha," she complains furiously. "Put me down!"

My mom steps out of the house as I carry her toward the garage. She's dressed in a black dress a little too short for her age. Her highlighted hair is fluffed up like a poodle and her makeup is caked on. She must have a date.

She stops on the top step and tilts her head to the side to get a better look. "Ella, is that you?"

Ella stops fussing and lifts up her head to look at my mom. "Hi, Miss Scott. How are you?"

"Hi, honey, I'm doing good... but is there a reason Micha's carrying you like that?" she questions. "Are you hurt?"

Ella shakes her head. "No, I'm fine. Micha just thinks he's funny."

Which means she secretly likes what I'm doing, but won't admit it.

"Actually, I'm taking her for a ride," I say slyly, inching my hand up the back of Ella's leg, and she slaps the back of my head playfully. "I'm taking you for a ride in my car. And you think I'm the pervert?"

My mom sighs, shaking her head, and opens her purse. "Well, it's nice to see you two together again." She takes out her car keys and her heels click as she trots down the steps. "Micha sure has missed you while you were gone."

"Bye mom," I wave her off, heading for the garage again, as my mom climbs into her Cadillac parked in the street near the curb.

"Is she going on a date?" Ella asks curiously.

"She's been going on a lot of dates lately." I swing open the car door and set her down in the passenger seat.

She tries to climb out. "I'm not going anywhere tonight Micha."

I gently push her back into the seat. "I'm not going to let you sit around in your room and sulk while your brother's around. Let's go out and have some fun."

She pauses, crossing her arms over her chest and her boobs nearly pop out of her top. "But I need to be there when Lila comes back. I can't just let her come back to Dean and my dad passed out on the couch."

"I'll take care of it." I rip my gaze from her tits, take out my cell phone, and text Ethan.

Me: Taking Ella up to The Back Road. Wanna get Lila and meet us up there?

Ella slumps back into the seat. "What are you up to?"

I hold up my finger. "Just a sec."

Ethan: Yeah, sounds cool.

Me: Is Lila up for it? And make sure u ask her. Don't just assume.

Ethan: She said she's good… but is Ella ok with going up there?

Me: We'll c when we get up there.

Ethan: Dude, she's gonna kick ur ass.

Me: C U there.

I stuff my phone into the back pocket of my jeans and close her door before climbing into the driver's seat.

"Where are you taking me?" she asks, trying to appear annoyed but her inquisitiveness seeps through her eyes.

"It's a surprise." Once the garage door is open, I peel down the driveway. "And Lila and Ethan are going to meet us there."

"A surprise, huh?" she mulls it over. "I'm not a fan of surprises."

My lips spread to a grin. "You're such a liar."

She stays silent and I know I've won this one, which is rare, but I'll take it. With a swift crank of the steering wheel, I align the car onto the road and spin the tires off into the night, happy because I managed to chip away a tiny piece of that armor she's wearing.

Chapter 8

Ella

I realize I have more issues than I thought. As soon as we turn onto the Back Road, a passion combusts inside me. It only flames hotter when we pull up to The Hitch, an old abandoned restaurant stationed at the end of the road.

It's the perfect set up for street racing, with a long straight road tucked between the lofty trees on the mountains. The sky is black, the moon bright, but there are clouds rolling in. I cringe, thinking of the night on the bridge. We'd been racing before I'd gone there.

Micha gets a text message right as we brink the end of the road. He pulls the car to the side, maneuvering carefully across the pot holes. He pushes the parking brake in and checks his phone, shutting it off, and looking torn up.

"What's wrong?" I ask. "You look upset?"

"Nothing's wrong. Everything's great." He's lying, but how can I press him to tell the truth when I'm a liar too?

"So this is your surprise?" I will my voice to sound disappointed, but it comes out pleased.

Micha gives me a sidelong glance. "Don't smile, pretty girl. It'll ruin your whole I'm-neutral-and-don't-give-a-shit act."

I opt to remain impartial. "Who are you planning to race tonight?"

"You mean who are *we* racing?" He smiles alluringly through the dark cab of the car. "Well, I thought I'd leave that up to you."

In front of the trees is a line of cars with their headlights on and their owners standing near the front. They're a rough crowd, mostly guys except for Shelia, a big girl with arms thicker than my legs. She's the only girl I've ever truly feared.

"Well, there's Mikey." I rub my forehead with the back of my hand. "Does he still got that piece of crap 6 cylinder in his Camaro?"

"Yeah, he does." Micha leans back in the seat, examining amusedly through the dark. "You think that's who I should go for?"

"It's the obvious choice." I don't like where my thoughts are heading, but I can't shut off my basic instinct. I've always been a hanging-out-with-the-guys kind of girl and therefor there is an abundance of knowledge about cars stashed away in my head. Lila is the first girl I've been friends with. "Although, what kind of a win would it be when you have this car that can clearly take on much more."

"You think I should take on someone in my own league?"

"If you want the win to mean anything, then yeah."

We look at each other, like magnets begging to get closer. Yet flip one the wrong direction and they will push apart.

"So which one is it, pretty girl?" He drapes an arm over the headrest behind me and his fingers brush my shoulder. "The underdog or the big dog."

There's a dare in the air, teasing the real me to come out tonight. I want to give in, just for a few hours, and let my inner ropes untie. I want to allow myself to breathe again, but I fear the loss of control—I fear I'll have to feel everything, including my guilt.

"Micha, I think we should go back." I put my seatbelt back on. "This isn't my thing anymore."

He presses his lips together firmly. "Please can we have a night? Just you and I. I really need this right now."

I pick up on his strange vibe and the sorrow in his eyes. "Okay, what's wrong? You've seemed a little out of it. Was it bad news on that text you got?"

He traces the figure eight tattoo on his forearm. "Do you remember when I got this?"

I absentmindedly touch my lower back. "How could I forget, since I have the same one on my back?"

"Do you remember why we got them?"

"I can't remember anything about that night."

"Exactly, yet you'll remember it forever. No matter what happens, which is completely ironic." He lets his finger linger on the tattoo that represents eternity.

"There's something bugging you." I tug the bottom of my shirt down to cover up my tattoo. "Do you want to talk about it?"

He shakes his head, still focused on the tattoo. "Nah, I'm good."

To distract him from his thoughts, I point my finger at a smokin' hot 1970 Pontiac GTO, blue with white racing stripes. "What about Benny? Does he still have the 455?"

Micha's eyes are pools of black liquid. "You think we should take on the big dog?"

"I think *you* should take on the big dog," I clarify. "I'll just watch you kick his ass."

His expression darkens. "No way. I'm not racing unless you're in the car with me. It's tradition."

A starvation inside me emerges. "Alright, I'll ride with you, just as long as you do one thing for me?"

"Say it and it's yours," he says without blinking.

My hunger urges me closer to him. I prop my elbows on the console, and my arms are trembling. He doesn't move, frozen like a statue as I put my lips next to his ear.

"Make sure you win," I breathe and my body arches into him on its own accord, before I sit back in the seat.

His face is indecipherable, his breathing fierce, his gaze relentless. "Okay, then. Let's go win us a race."

We climb out of the car and hike across the dirt road toward the row of cars and their owners. I shield my eyes from the headlights and wrap an arm around myself, knowing these guys are going to give me crap for how I'm dressed.

Micha swings his arm around me protectively. "Relax. I got you baby."

"Well, what do we have here?" Mikey, the owner of the Camaro, strides up to us. He's got black hair, a kink in his nose, and his thick neck is enclosed with a barb-wire tattoo. "Is the infamous duo back again to get their asses kicked?"

I roll my eyes. "You beat us once and that was by default due to a flat tire."

His face pinches as he takes in my shirt, tank top, and curled hair. "What the fuck happened to you?"

Chandra, his girlfriend, sputters a laugh. Her dress is so tight that her curves bulge out of it and her stilettoes make her almost the same height as me. "Holy shit, she like turned into a little princess or something."

Micha squeezes my shoulder, trying to keep me calm. "So who's up first? Or has no one decided yet."

Mikey eyes Micha's Chevelle and there's a nervous look in his eyes. "You think you can just walk in here and play the game after sitting out for nearly a year?"

I mouth to Micha, *a year*?

Micha shrugs. "What? You were gone. Why the hell would I want to race?"

"Again, you need to move on without…" I trail off. Mikey will use what I say against Micha, so I have to watch my mouth. "We want to race Benny."

Mikey's laughter echoes the night. "You and what army?"

I point at Micha's Chevelle parked near the road. "That army right there."

Mikey shakes his head and shoos us away. "That thing don't stand a chance against the GTO. Now run along and come back when you got something bigger."

He's testing my control. A lot.

"As opposed to yours?" I retort, getting into Mikey's face. "Because that thing's all looks and no go."

Micha directs me back by the shoulders and a trace of amusement laces his voice. "Easy there, tiger. Let's try not to get our asses kicked tonight, okay?"

Benny hops off the hood of his car, flicks his cigarette to the ground, and leaves his buddies to join us. "What's up? Did I hear someone wanted to race me?"

Benny's the kind of guy that everyone respects because they're afraid of him. When he was a freshman he got into a fight at school with a senior twice his size and beat him up pretty badly. No one knows what the fight was over or what happened, but it was enough that everyone became cautious of Benny.

Mikey points a finger sharply at me. "Princess right here wants to challenge you to a race in that thing."

Benny's eyes wander to the Chevelle as he cocks his shaven head and crosses his muscular arms. "Micha, isn't that your car?"

Micha pats my back and winks at me. "Yeah, apparently she's my spokesperson."

Benny deliberates this and then turns to Mikey, who's glaring at me. "I don't see what the big deal is. I have no problem with Micha racing. In fact, it might be kinda nice to have a challenge for a change." Benny slaps Mikey on the back kind of hard and then pounds fists with Micha.

"Thanks man," Micha says with a respective nod. "Are you and I going to line up first then?"

Benny bobs his head up and down, nodding as he stares at the road pensively. "Yeah man, I think that'd work."

Jessica Sorensen

They chat a little bit more about the rules and what not, while Mikey continues to scowl at me like an angry dog. Once they're done talking, Micha and I walk back to the car, while everyone else scatters toward the starting line located right in front of The Hitch.

"So what's your plan?" I ask. "Because beating him won't be easy."

"You're my plan." He opens the passenger door for me. "With you in the car, there's no way I won't win, otherwise you'll never let me live it down."

Tucking my head into the car, I drop into the seat and then look up at him. "I won't make your car go any faster."

He grins, slamming the door. "Sure you will." He slides across the front of the hood and climbs into the driver's seat.

"You're such a show off," I remark.

He starts up the engine and it thunders to life. "That's like the pot calling the kettle black."

I slump back in the seat and fold my arms. "I may have been a lot of things, but I was never a show off."

He hooks a finger under my chin and angles my head toward him. "Taylor Crepner's graduation party two years ago. You were standing on the roof with a snowboard strapped to your feet, telling everyone you could make the jump. I think that's pretty close to showing off."

133

I make an innocent face. "But I did make the jump, didn't I?"

"Yeah, but not without breaking your arm," he says. "And that's beside the point."

"You're right," I admit, touching the small scar on my arm where the bone broke through the skin. "I was showing off and you had to drive my dumb ass to the hospital, then sit in the waiting room while I had surgery to put my arm back together."

His finger traces a line down my neck and to my chest bone. "I was there because I wanted to be."

"You missed a performance because of me."

"I don't care—never have."

My gaze involuntarily flicks to his lips. Suddenly, I want to kiss him, like I did that night on the bridge. It makes me uncomfortable because the feeling owns me. I lean away, putting space between us. Sensing my transfer of attitude, he revs up the engine and spins the tires, fishtailing the car to the startup line.

He shoots me a smug look, cocking an eyebrow. "Now that's showing off."

Shaking my head, I restrain a grin. Benny lines up the front of his GTO with Micha's Chevelle and his girlfriend struts up between the two cars. She's wearing jeans and a short t-shirt that shows her stomach. She flips her dark hair off her shoulder and then raises her hands above her head. People line up along the road, watching, and placing bets on the winner.

I spot Ethan and Lila toward the front, chatting about something, and Lila is doing her flirty hair flip thing. "When did they get here?"

Micha ignores me, eyeing Benny through his rolled down window. "To the baseline and back?"

Benny's arm is resting casually on top of the steering wheel. "Yeah, man. First one back wins."

They look away from each other. Benny waves at his girlfriend and she nods her head.

"On your mark. Get set. Go!" Her hands shoot down and screeches cut the air. A trail of dust engulfs us as we race off. The trees on the side of the road are a blur, and the sky is one big streak of stars. I keep silent as Micha shifts the car over and over again, but something inside me awakens from a very deep sleep.

Benny pulls ahead and makes a sharp swerve right in front of us. His red tail lights are blinding in the night and his exhaust is puffing out thin clouds of smoke. Micha speeds up, inching the front end toward the rear of the GTO.

As we approach the end, Benny pulls farther ahead but it's not over yet. Micha has a thing for flipping the car around, without decreasing the acceleration. It's scary as hell, but it works every time. Besides with the longer body of Benny's GTO it doesn't have quite the turning power.

We reach the end and I should probably be nervous. The road cuts off into a steep, rocky hill and the space to turn around is narrow, but I've never gotten scared, not even now. I guess I can't change what's in my blood.

The GTO begins to slant sideways as Benny turns it. Micha veers to the side to get around him and shoots for the open gap between the car and the trees. I grab the handle above my head, the brakes squeal, and I brace my feet up on the dashboard. It's like being on a merry-go-round on crack. Everything spins—the trees, the sky, Micha. For a second, I shut my eyes and it feels like I'm flying. It takes me back to the night on the bridge. *She said she could fly.*

The car straightens out and Micha floors the gas pedal. Like I predicted, Benny is having a harder time lining back up. By the time we're speeding up the road again, he's a small distance behind us. Micha punches the gas and shifts the car into a higher gear.

The long front end of the GTO materializes through my window and Micha floors it, shooting me a look that lets me know I can tell him to slow down if I want.

I don't.

People flee to the side, panicking at our dangerous speed as we rip through the finish line. It isn't clear who the winner is or who's going to be able to get their car to

stop in time, before crushing into The Hitch. Brakes shriek
and dust swamps the windows. My body is thrown forward with the car's abrupt halt and I smack my head on
the dashboard.

Micha works to regain control of the wheel and
straightens the car as it skids to a stop. Everything settles
and the dust slowly clears. Micha and I stare out the windshield, breathing loudly, our eyes as wide as golf balls. The
front bumper of the Chevelle is a sliver away from a very
large tree.

"Holy shit," Micha whispers and looks at me, his eyes
bulging. "Are you okay?"

I lower my hand from the dashboard, my chest heav-
ing with my breaths. Rubbing the bump on my head, I
turn in my seat toward Micha. There is an eerie calm inside me and one of my worst fears becomes a reality. I'm
an adrenaline junkie. Plain and simple, but I think it's how
I've been all along. I just never admitted.

I'm no longer in control.

As I incline toward Micha, my heart flutters to life in
my chest. My eyes shut and my lips brush his, gently tasting him. It feeds my hunger vaguely and I edge back,
letting my eyes open. Micha is looking at me, his eyes
pools of blue like the deep spots of the ocean hidden from
the world. His hand comes up behind my head and he en-
tices my lips back to his.

Something snaps inside me, like a rubber band. With one swift movement, and the aid of my own willingness, Micha lifts me over the console and I straddle his lap, looping my arms around his neck. His hands burrow into my thighs and slip under my skirt onto my bare skin. My breath falters at the intimacy of his touch. No one has ever touched me like this before, without me running away. Usually, being this close to someone sends me into a room packed with self-doubt, panic, distrust, and unfamiliarity.

My legs tense and Micha leans back. "Stay here, baby," he whispers, like he can read my thoughts. "Trust me, okay? Don't run."

He waits for me to nod and then crashes his lips into mine, keeping his hands under my skirt. I arch my body into him, pressing my chest against his, and my nipples tingle. His tongue sensually plays with mine, tracing every spot on my mouth and my lips. My body starts to fill with a secret longing.

Micha moves his mouth away from mine and my legs tremble in objection. He sucks a path of kisses down my jawline, moving to my neck and residing on my chest right above where my breast curves out of the top of my shirt. It sends a shock through my body and my legs uncontrollably tighten around him, my knees pressing into his sides.

He lets out a slow, deep groan and his hand slides higher into my skirt as he guides me closer. I can feel him pressing in between my legs and it scares the shit out of me, but not enough to make me stop. It's like all the sexual tension I ran away from has sprung free all at once. My fingers sneak under the bottom of his shirt and trace along the outline of his lean muscles. I don't know where to stop or how to put the line back up. My mind is racing and I clutch onto his shoulders needing my control back.

Someone bangs on the window. "Are you two having fun in there?"

I jump back and my cheeks start to heat at the sight of Ethan and Lila staring at us through the window. In his black tee and jeans, Ethan blends in with the night, but his dark, insinuating smile glows. Lila's eyes are magnified and her jaw is hanging open. Micha does nothing to help the situation. A lazy grin spreads across his face as he watches me through hooded eyes, looking very pleased with himself.

The adrenaline washes out of me and leaves a numb feeling in its place. I climb off his lap and straighten my skirt and hair before getting out of the car. I calmly walk around the back of the car and join Ethan and Lila.

"So who won the race?" I ask, smoothing the last of the wrinkles out of my skirt.

Ethan smirks at me. "Is that what you're really thinking about at the moment?"

I stare at him blankly. "What else would I be thinking about?"

Micha climbs out of the car, stretching his long legs. "We won, I'm pretty sure," he says, taking my hand like it's the most natural thing in the world. "Although, I'm betting there's an argument going on about it."

Ethan nods agreeably and takes a sip of his soda. "Yep, everyone who bet on you is insisting you've won and vice-versa with Benny."

Micha interlaces our fingers. "So the same old, same old."

"You know how these things go." Ethan pats Micha's shoulder sympathetically. "They're never going to come to a decision."

My hand is sweating in Micha's. He just cracked me open and my mind is racing with a billion thoughts. I can't do this with him. I can't crush him. I need to repaint the lines somehow.

"We should just leave," Micha says to me. "Let's not even give them the benefit of our argument."

"You want to drive out of here all suave?" I ask. "And make a grand exit?"

Micha smiles and squeezes my hand. "A grand statement."

"Which would be?"

"That we don't give a shit."

I let out a shaky breath and nod. "That sounds good to me."

"You want to meet up at the house?" he asks Ethan. "I'm sure we're going to have to do some tuning up on The Beast after what I just did."

Lila scrunches her nose and pops her gum. "The beast? Do I even want to know what that is?"

Micha taps the car door with his free hand. "Yep, that's what I named it. Kind of like how you call your car your baby."

Lila laughs. "Oh, I get it. Although, I like my name better."

Micha traces his thumb along the palm of my hand. "Are you ready to go? Or do you want to go pick a fight with someone first."

I flash a panicked glance at Lila, who knits her eyebrows. "Maybe Lila and I should ride together. I haven't spent any time with her today."

"You've spent time with me every day for the last eight months," she replies. "I think we're good for a few hours."

"I'll take care of her." Ethan chucks the empty bottle of soda across the parking lot and it lands in the back of his truck. "Really, really good care of her."

Lila lets her blonde hair fall into her face to hide her blush. I've never seen her blush like that. What exactly have the two of them been up to tonight?

Micha shakes his head at Ethan. "Be good."

Ethan rolls his eyes and then walks off with Lila toward his truck. Micha and I get into his car and I prepare myself to make a speech.

Micha squeezes his eyes shut and holds his hand up. "Don't even say it. Just let it go for the night. Please. I need to just feel this."

The pain in his voice causes me to fasten my jaw shut. Opening his eyes, he starts up the car and we drive down the road. Micha waves to Benny as we pass and everyone's eyes follow us. Then the darkness takes over as we pull out onto the main road and the headlights light up the night like a tunnel that leads to the unknown.

Chapter 9

Micha

I've slept in my own bed for the past week, even though my body itched to do another maneuver up the tree and into Ella's window. She's been avoiding me ever since we made out in my car. I'm guessing she needs some time to sort through her thoughts; that I was overwhelming her.

Ella has always had issues with intimacy and pushed people away, including me if I try to cross the friend line. I actually had to work to become her friend. We've always lived next door, but it took me bribing her with a juice box and a toy car to even get her to let me climb over the fence into her yard.

But it was worth the time. Fifteen years later, we're still friends. I can't imagine my life without her, something I grasped that night when I found her on the bridge. Even though I knew she wasn't going to jump, seeing her standing on the ledge made me realize that I want and need her in my life forever. She challenges me, pushes me, and pisses me off, but I wouldn't have it any other way.

It's late in the afternoon when I wake up. Blinking against the bright sun, I drag my butt out of bed and throw on an old tee and some jeans. Ethan and I are still working on fixing the blown head gasket on my car, so I send him a text that I'm up and ready to go. I head into the kitchen and drink the orange juice straight out of the jug.

My mom walks in combing her hair, and scolds me. "Micha Scott, how many times have I told you not to do that crap?" She snatches the juice away and sets it back in the fridge.

I wipe away the juice from my chin. "I think it's called selective hearing."

She does up the buttons on her jacket, dressed to head off to her day job as a secretary at the dealership. She also has a night job as a hostess at a café. "You are such a smart ass." She holds up a red lacy bra. "Okay, so I know I've always been the cool mom, but finding this in my bed is crossing the line."

"Isn't it yours?" I grab a box of cereal out of the cupboard.

She scowls at me as she tosses the bra into the trash behind her. "I have much more class than that."

Thinking of her trashy dress the other night, I can't help but laugh. "That's breaking news to me."

She gently slaps the back of my head and I laugh, rubbing it like it hurts. "If you must know, I had a date that night with a really nice guy, but he's a little younger than me and I was trying to make a good first impression."

"So that's why you had that trashy dress on." I scoop a handful of cereal out of the box and stuff it into my mouth. "I was wondering about that."

"I didn't look that bad," she protests, grabbing her keys from the hook on the wall. "Did I?"

I hate it when she asks questions like these; ones that don't have a right answer. I shrug and put the cereal back into the cupboard.

She grabs a granola bar out of the cupboard. "So Ella's back for good I'm guessing?"

I crunch slowly on the cereal. "Yeah, until summer's over."

She waits for me to embellish. "Are you going to tell me where she was for the last eight or nine months?"

"College," I say. "In Vegas."

"Wow, I'm actually impressed with that answer." She peels the wrapper off the granola bar. "Good for her."

I frown. "Why? She bailed on everyone."

"I'm not saying how she did it was right, but it's good she's going somewhere in her life."

"I told you I have plans. I just need to figure out a way to make them happen."

She sighs and pats my head like I'm still a child. "I worry about you spending too much time chasing her. You might have to realize that maybe she doesn't want to get caught, sweetie. Trust me. It was something I had to learn with your dad." She hangs her bag over her shoulder and drums her fingernails on the counter. "Micha, did you think about what I told you the other night?"

"You mean with that random text you sent me?"

She sighs heavy-heartedly. "I'm sorry I broke the news to you like that. It's been sitting on my chest for a while and I just couldn't figure out a way to do it. I panicked." She hangs her head. "I'm a terrible mother, aren't I?"

I shake my head and give her a hug because I can sense she needs one. "Being a terrible news breaker doesn't make you a terrible mother. I've always had a roof over my head and food to eat."

She hugs me back. "Yeah, but sometimes it feels like I should have spent more time with you. I mean, every mother in the world gives more than what I do."

My eyes travel over her head to the window. Ella's house is right outside, looking broken and beaten. "Not every mother. In fact, some can't help not to."

She steps away, wiping her eyes with the back of her hand. "Are you going to call him?"

I eye my father's number tacked to the wall next to the phone. "I haven't decided yet."

She dabs her fingers under her eyes, fixing her makeup. "Just make sure to think about it from both sides. I know he's been out of your life for forever, but he sounded genuine on the phone. I think he really wants to see you."

I force a smile. "Alright, I'll think about it."

My father bailed out when I was six and we haven't heard from him since. My mom went looking for him right after he left, but she came back telling me she couldn't find him. I've always wondered if she did find him, but didn't want to tell me the truth.

My mom leaves the house and I relax on the couch with my feet kicked up on the table as I wait around for Ethan to show up. I'm surfing through the channels when the home phone rings.

"Hello."

"Umm... is this Micha?" A voice responds.

"Yeah... why? Who's this?"

A long pause fills the connection and I think I've lost the weirdo.

"Are you there?" I ask, getting annoyed.

"Yeah." He clears his throat. "This is your father."

I nearly drop the damn phone.

"Micha, this is you, isn't it?" He sounds old and formal and it pisses me off.

"Yeah it's me," I say through gritted teeth.

"I know your mother was going to have you call me, but there is something I need to talk to you about," he says. "And it can't wait."

I consider his request. "I've been waiting almost fourteen years to talk to you. I think you can wait a little bit longer." Then I slam the phone down and punch the wall.

The sheetrock crumbles to the counter top and the hook holding the keys crashes to the floor.

"Fuck!" I collapse to the ground, hoping no one walks in and sees me falling apart.

Especially Ella.

Chapter 10

Ella

I can remember the first time I wanted to kiss Micha as clearly as the day I found my mother dead. Both times were equally as terrifying, but in two different ways.

Micha and I had been sitting on the hood of his car at our secret spot tucked away in the trees, staring out at the lake. It was harder than hell to get back to the spot, but the view and serenity made it worth it.

It had been quiet between the two of us for a while, which was normal except for the jealousy stirring inside me over Micha's latest hook up, Cassandra. I'd never felt this way before and it puzzled me. It wasn't like the girl was anything special to Micha, but he'd told Ethan that she had the potential to be girlfriend material and it was bugging me.

Micha's arms were tucked under his head and his eyes were shut as the sunlight beamed down on him. His shirt had ridden up and I could see his tattoo peeking out. As I stared at it the urge to run my fingers along it drove me crazy.

"I don't like Cassandra," I abruptly sputtered out, sitting up quickly.

Micha's eyebrows knitted as his eyes gradually opened against the sunlight. "Huh?"

"That Cassandra girl you were talking about the other day," I said, staring out at the water rippling in the gentle breeze. "I don't think you should date her."

He rose up on his elbows. "Because you don't like her?"

"No..." I tucked strands of my auburn hair out of my eyes. "I just don't want you to date her."

The wind filled the silence. Micha sat up and wrapped an arm around my shoulder.

"Okay, I won't," he said as if it was as simple as breathing.

I pressed back a smile, not fully understanding why the hell I was so happy. Micha lay back down and drew me with him. I rested my head on his chest and listened to his heart beating, steady as a rock, unlike mine which was dancing inside my chest.

The longer I stayed in his arms, the more content I became. I felt safe, like nothing could hurt me, but I was in complete denial that I was starting to fall in love with my best friend.

***

It's been a week since the car racing incident and I've been hiding out in my bedroom living on mac n' cheese and Diet Dr. Pepper. Dean still hasn't headed home, but Lila did the morning after the race. She wanted to stay, but I didn't want her to and I think her dad wasn't too keen on the idea either.

It's been kind of lonely, though.

I still haven't listened to Micha's voicemail, and the constant flashing on the screen torments me. I decide to take a break from the house today and do something I've been meaning to do for a while. I want to sketch my mother's grave because I won't always be close enough to visit it. It's been bothering me the entire eight months that I've been gone. I feel guilty because it was me who put her there and then I just left her.

I collect my sketch book and pencils from the drawer of my night stand, slip on my shoes and sunglasses, and head out the front door where I'm less likely to run into Micha. It's a warm day and the blue sky glitters with sunshine. I walk up the sidewalk toward Cherry Hill and decide to make a last minute stop at Grady's.

I knock on the trailer door and Amy, the nurse, answers it wearing blue scrubs. "Oh, hi Ella, I don't think Grady's up for any visitors today, sweetie."

"But he told me to stop by," I say stupidly. "I know it's a little later than I told him and I'm sorry."

"He's not mad at you, Ella," she says kindly. "I've just got him hooked up on oxygen and he's got a cough."

I shield my eyes from the sun and stare up at her. "Is he okay?"

She sighs, leaning against the doorframe. "He's just having a rough day today, but try back in a few days, okay hun."

I nod and back down the steps as she shuts the door. I stare helplessly at the back window which leads to Grady's room. He's sick and there's nothing I can do. I have no control over this. Micha was right. I can't control everything.

As horrid images of my mom's death flash through my mind, I run into the field and throw up.

***

The town's cemetery is located up on Cherry Hill, which on foot is quite a hike, but I enjoy the break from the reality of life. There is no one up there—there hardly ever is. I push through the gate and situate by a tree right in front of my mom's headstone. It's a small cemetery bordered by trees and the grass is covered with dry leaves.

As I sketch the lines of the fence and the vines that coil it, I angle downward and draw the curve of her tombstone. I become lost in the movements, adding wings to the side of it, because she was always so fascinated with flying.

152

A few weeks before her death, my mother begged me to go on a walk with her. I gave in even though I had plans that day. It was sunny and the air smelled like cut grass. It felt like nothing could go wrong.

She wanted to go to the bridge so we walked all the way across town to the lake. When we arrived there, she climbed on the railing and spread her hands out to balance as her long auburn hair flapped in the wind.

"Mom, what are you doing?" I said, reaching for the back of her shirt to pull her down.

She sidestepped down the railing out of my reach and stared at the water below. "Ella May, I think I can fly."

"Mom, stop it and get down," I said, not taking her very seriously at first.

But when she turned her head and looked at me, I could see in her eyes that she wasn't joking. She really believed she could fly.

I tried to stay as composed as possible. "Mom, please get down. You're scaring me."

She shook her head and her legs wobbled a little. "It's okay honey. I'll be fine. I can feel it in my body that I can fly."

I took a cautious step toward her and my foot bumped the curb of the bridge. The cement rubbed my toe raw and I could feel blood oozing out, but I didn't look down at it. I was too afraid to take my eyes off her. "Mom, you can't fly. *People* can't fly."

"Then maybe I'm a bird," she said seriously. "Maybe I have wings and feathers and they can carry me away and I can become one with the wind."

"You're not a bird!" I shouted and reached for her again, but she hopped onto one of the beams and laughed like it was a game. I tugged my fingers through my hair and steadied onto the railing. It was a far fall, one that would crush our bodies on impact, even in the water. I braced my hands on the beams above my head. "Mom, if you love me at all, you'll get down."

She shook her head. "No, I'm going to fly today."

A truck rolled up and stopped on the middle of the bridge as I edged toward her. Ethan jumped out and didn't so much as flinch at the scenario. "Hey, Mrs. Daniels. How's it going?"

I gaped at him and hissed, "What are you doing?"

He ignored me. "You know it's not really safe out there."

My mom angled her head to the side. "I think I'll be okay. My wings will carry me away."

I was mortified, but Ethan didn't miss a beat. He rested his arms on the railing. "As much as that could be true, what if it's not? Then what? I mean is it really worth the risk?"

I glanced back at my mom and she looked like she was weighing the options. She stared at the dark water below her feet and then at the bright sky above her head. "Maybe I should think about it for a little bit."

Ethan nodded. "I think that's probably a good idea."

She made a path across the beam and planted her feet on the railing. Ethan helped her down and we got her into the backseat of his truck. She fell asleep within minutes and I slumped my head back against the chair.

"How did you do that?" I asked quietly.

"One of my friends was tripping out of their mind one night and I had to talk him out of jumping off the roof," he explained. "It was all about making her realize that there was more than one scenario."

I nodded and we stayed quiet for the rest of the drive to my house. Ethan never brought it up to me, nor did he treat me differently and I was grateful for it.

After a doctor's visit, it was determined that my mother had started to suffer from 'Delusions of Grandeur,' which happens sometimes in bipolar patients.

I finally pull away from the drawing when it's nearly dark. I gather my sketchpad and pencils and head down the hill. In front of the arch iron entryway is Micha, sitting on the hood of his mom's car, wearing jeans, and a black and red plaid shirt. His head is tipped down and wisps of his blonde hair cover his forehead as he messes around with his phone.

I stop a little ways off from him. "What are you doing here?"

His eyes lift from his phone. "I'm waiting for you."

"How did you know I was here?"

"I saw you leave with your sketchpad and head this way, so I came up to check on you."

I take a tentative step forward. "How long have you been sitting here?"

He slides off the hood and puts his phone away. "For a while, but I didn't want to disturb you. You looked too peaceful."

I press my lips together and stare at him, craving to sketch him like I used to. He would sit on my bed and it was like he owned my hand. "Look, about the other night, I think—"

He strides across the grass toward me, moving so impulsively that there's no time to react as his finger covers my lips. "Just let it be for a while, okay?"

Uncertain of his exact meaning, I nod anyway.

He lets his finger fall from my lips, trailing a line down my chest, finally pulling away at the bottom of my stomach. "You want a ride home?" His voice comes out ragged.

I glance at the grey sky and the birds flying across it. "That would be nice. Thank you."

Micha

She's preoccupied during the drive and so am I. I was so pissed off about my father that I got into the car about to do something reckless, however, then I saw Ella wandering down the street, and I followed her. The way she walked was very entertaining, her auburn hair blowing in the wind, and the way she swayed her ass in the short denim shorts she was wearing. It calmed me down watching her sit up on the hill and draw, but I can't stop thinking about the phone conversation.

"We should go somewhere," I announce when we drive onto the main road.

Ella jolts in her seat and turns away from the window. "I should probably go home."

"Come on." I pout, hoping it'll win her over. "Just come with me somewhere and we can relax."

She's tempted. "Where exactly?"

I turn the volume of the stereo down and let my arm rest on the top of the steering wheel. "To our spot by the lake."

"But it takes forever to get there." Her eyes rise to the dark sky. "And it's getting late."

"Since when have you been afraid of the dark?"

"It's not the dark I'm afraid of."

I sigh and downshift. "Come on, just you and me. We don't even have to talk. We can just sit in silence."

"Fine," she surrenders, tossing her sketchpad into the backseat. "Just as long as you don't ask me questions."

I hold up my hand innocently. "Scouts honor. I'll keep my questions to myself."

Her eyes narrow. "I know you've never been in the scouts before."

I laugh, feeling the pressure lift from my chest. "It doesn't matter. I'll keep my questions to myself, but with everything else, all bets are off."

She pretends to have an itch on her nose, but really it's to obscure her smile and it makes me smile myself.

***

Its pitch black by the time we reach our spot on the shore that's secluded by tall trees. The moon reflects against the water and the night air is a little chilly. I get my jacket out of the trunk and offer it to Ella, knowing she's cold because of the goosebumps on her arms and the way her nipples are poking through her shirt.

158

She slips the jacket on and zips it up, covering up her perky nipples. I sigh, hop onto the hood, and open my arms for her to join me. Hesitantly, she climbs onto the hood, but stays at the front, with her feet propped up on the bumper, gazing out at the water.

I scoot down by her and keep my knees up, resting my elbows on them. "What are you thinking about?"

Her eyes are huge in the moonlight. "Death."

"What about death?" I wonder if we're finally going to go back to that night.

"That Grady's going to die," she whispers softly. "And there's nothing I can do about it."

I brush her hair back from her forehead. "You need to stop worrying about everything that can't be controlled."

She sighs and leans away from my hand. "That's just it, though. It's *all* I can think about anymore. It's like this fixation I have no control over which makes no sense because I'm fixated on controlling the uncontrollable." She's breathing wildly.

Shit. I need to calm her down.

"Hey, come here." I loop my arms around her waist and lie her down on the windshield with me. She rests her head on my chest and I play with her hair, breathing in her vanilla scent. "Do you remember when you decided that it would be a good idea if you climbed up the scaffolding in the gym?"

"I wanted to prove to Gary Bennitt that I was as tough as the boys." She buries her face into my shirt, ashamed. "Why do you remember everything?"

"How could I forget that? You scared the hell out of me when you fell. Yet, somehow you managed to land on the board just below it."

"I thought I was going to die," she murmurs. "I was so stupid."

"You weren't stupid, you just saw life at a different angle," I say. "I've always envied you for it. Like when you used to dance in a room where no one was dancing or how you stuck up for people. But there was always that wall you put up. You would never let anyone completely through."

She's soundless for a while and I expect for her to push me away. But she sits up and hovers over me, her hair veiling our faces. Her breath is ragged, like she's terrified out of her mind.

"I opened up to you once," she whispers. "When we were here in this spot doing this same thing."

I can't take my eyes off her lips. "I'm not sure what you're talking about."

She licks her lips. "I told you I didn't want you dating Cassandra."

"Cassandra... Oh, was that what that was about?" I start to laugh.

"What's so funny?" she asks, but I can't stop laughing. She pinches my nipple and I jerk upward, smacking my forehead against hers. "*Ow.*" She blinks, rubbing her forehead and a laugh escapes her lips. "Tell me what's so fun-funny."

She looks beautiful, trying to be pissed, when deep down she's relishing the moment. I'm enjoying myself, which I didn't envisage tonight, but if anyone can cheer me up, it's her. Like when my dad left and she caught me in the garage, clutching onto his tool box crying like a baby. She gave me her Popsicle and then just sat there with me until I ran out of tears.

I eye her over and she fusses with her hair self-consciously. With one swift movement, I flip us over so my body is covering hers. "When I told Ethan about that day when you told me not to see Cassandra, he told me you had a thing for me. He's usually not right about those things."

"I didn't have a thing for you," she argues. "I just didn't want anyone else to have a thing for you."

"You're adorable when you deny the truth. You always have been."

"Micha, I used to have studs on every item of clothing I owned and enough black eyeliner to make an entire sketch. That's not adorable."

"It is on you." I wink at her.

She shakes her head and pokes a finger at my chest. "Don't try and use your player moves on me."

We remain silent, frozen in the moment, until I finally speak again. "I have an idea." Curiosity slowly takes over her face as I shift over her body. My arms are at the side of her head, barely holding my weight up. My face hovers above hers, our lips only an inch apart, and she lies perfectly still. "I want to kiss you."

She shakes her head promptly. "I don't think that's a good idea."

I trace one of my fingers over her lips. I've been going about this all wrong. I can't force myself on her. I have to move slow and think of her as a skittish cat that needs to be approached cautiously.

"Just kiss. I swear to God that's all we'll do." I move my finger away from her lips. "And kissing's not that scary, right?"

"With you it is," she says truthfully.

"If you want me not to, just say it." Taking my time, I leisurely lower my lips toward hers.

She stays stationary, her big green eyes targeted on my mouth. Slowly, so she has time to let her thoughts slow down, I caress my lips across hers. A small gasp flees from her lips and I slip my tongue into her mouth. Her hands glide up my back and into my hair. My body conforms to hers as I explore her mouth with my tongue. She bites

162

down on my bottom lip, sucking my lip ring into her mouth before releasing it.

Fuck. She's making this hard. I intensify the kiss as my body becomes more impatient, but I keep my promise and only kiss her, even when she fastens her legs around my waist and rubs up against me.

Ella

He said just kiss and it seemed okay, but now my body has developed a mind of its own. I'm writhing my hips against him enjoying the pleasure erupting inside me. He's hard between my legs as he kisses me so fiercely that my lips are swollen. His fingers tangle in my hair and his tongue plunges deeper and deeper into my mouth the more I rock against him. My head falls back and my eyes open to the stars shining in the sky. It feels like I'm falling or flying... I'm not sure, but whatever it is I can't seem to control it. For a second, I want to capture the moment, put it in a jar, and always have it with me, but panic seizes my mind and I jerk away from his lips.

His eyes snap open and his pupils are vast. "What's wrong?"

"Nothing... It's just... I have to calm down." I take a deep breath, my skin still tingling in the spots his hands touched.

Micha nods, breathless. Carefully, he moves off of me and leans back against the window, securing his hand around mine. We don't speak as we stare up at the sky. He traces his finger along the folds between my fingers and my eyelids drift shut. I feel a wall crumble, leaving behind dust, debris, and pieces that desperately need to be put back together.

***

"Are you okay?" I ask Micha when we pull into my driveway. He's been quiet the whole drive home and I can tell something's bothering him.

"Yeah, I'm fine," he says with a shrug and then his gaze darts to the back window as headlights shine up behind us. "Although, you might not be."

My eyebrows furrow. "Why? What's wrong?"

He points a finger at a car parking at the curb in front of my house; a shiny black Mercedes with a familiar blonde-haired driver sitting in it.

"Oh my God, is that Lila's car?" I ask.

"I'm guessing yes, since I doubt anyone around here owns a Mercedes."

Lila climbs out of the car and it's clear that she's been crying. Her eyes are swollen and her cheeks are red. She has her pajama bottoms on and a hoodie pulled over her head. The last time she walked around in an outfit like that she'd just broken up with her boyfriend.

"I think she might have some issues at home," I tell him, grabbing the door handle. "She acted like she didn't want to go home."

"But you didn't ask her about it?" he questions with an arch of his eyebrow.

I bite my lip guiltily. "I wasn't sure I wanted to know the answer." God, I'm a terrible friend.

Lila heads up the driveway and we get out to meet her around the back. Before I can say anything, she hugs me and starts to sob. I tense, not used to being hugged, except by Micha.

"I didn't want to go back there," she cries. "I knew this was going to happen."

I look over Lila's head at Micha for help. "It'll be okay."

He gives me a sympathetic look and mouths, *take her inside.*

I nod and he waves at me, getting back into his car. I guide Lila into the house holding her weight up for her like she's ill. When I get her into my room, she curls up on my bed and hugs a pillow.

I wait a minute before I speak. "Do you want to talk about it?"

She shakes her head. "I just want to go to sleep."

"Alright." I turn off the light and collapse onto the trundle. I need to get into my pajamas, but it's been an exhausting day.

"My dad hates me," Lila whispers through sobs.

I freeze and then sit up, squinting at her through the dark. "I'm sure he doesn't hate you."

"Yes, he does," she says. "He always says so—that he wished he had sons instead of daughters because they're easier to deal with."

"Are you going to be okay?" I ask, unsure what else to say.

"I will be. It'll just take some time."

Was that the magical cure? Time. I flop back down and fall asleep to the murmur of her sobs.

Chapter 11

Ella

The next morning Lila is feeling much better. It's like last night never happened, but I wonder if it's an act.

"I have a feeling that today is going to be full of rainbows and sunshine," Lila says cheerily as she applies her lipstick, using the mirror on the closet door.

Against my protest, she took down some of my sketches, so she could see her reflection. "See what, though?" I'd asked and she laughed, totally confused.

"Are you high?" I tease as I twist my hair onto the back of my head and secure it with a clip.

She pauses, looking at me over her shoulder. "Why do you always ask questions like that?"

I slip on my boots and tie up the laces. "What kinds of questions?"

She blots her lips. "Every time I'm happy, you always ask if I'm drunk or on something. People can be happy without substances."

I clasp a watch around my wrist. "Most people can, but not all."

Lila clips a diamond earring in. "You look really nice today."

I glance down at the black and purple dress I have on and the boots on my feet. "I forgot to do laundry so I had to wear some of my old clothes, which don't match any of my new shoes."

"Well you look nice." She gives an elongated pause. "So what's on the agenda for today?"

"It depends on what you're doing?" I ask. "Are you… where are you planning on staying?"

She shuts off her phone and then discards it onto the bed. "I'd like to stick around with you for a while, if you don't mind. We could hang out. I don't have anything scheduled for the summer and I'm not going back home."

"Do you want to tell me what happened?"

"No, not really."

"Okay… well, I need to find a job," I say. "I have to save up for the rest of my tuition since it doesn't look like I'll be getting that internship."

She puts a headband in her hair. "The one at that art museum."

"That's the one and it doesn't start until mid-June," I explain. "But that's only five weeks away, so I figured they'd have notified me if I got it."

"You never know. Sometimes things like that move slow." She folds up a shirt and packs it into her bag, then ties a ribbon on the back of her shirt. "Although, if you get it that'd mean you'd have to go back to Vegas, right?"

Nodding, I head for the door. Two weeks ago the idea of returning to the desert would make me happy, but something's changed. I still want to go, though leaving will be a little bit harder.

I collect my phone off the dresser, noting the flashing voicemail on the screen—Micha's unread message. My finger hovers above the button as I step into the hall. He told me I wasn't ready for what was on it? But am I ready for it now?

"I don't know why you think it's so bad here." Lila follows me. "Yeah, people are a little rough, but they're not all bad and everywhere has bad stuff. You can't hide from it."

"That's very insightful." I close my phone and put it away.

"Bad comes in different forms," Lila continues. "Whether it's drug dealers on the corner or if it's corrupt rich people or just your run-of-the-mill douche bag."

I don't know much about Lila, other than she's rich, her dad works as a lawyer and her mom stays home. She likes clothes, is great with numbers and was the only reason I passed pre-calculus.

My brother's door is open and he walks out as we're passing by. He has a black and red polo shirt on and a pair of cargo pants. There's some kind of gel in his hair and it looks shiny.

"Hey, have you seen dad?" he asks, giving an acknowledging glance at Lila.

I point at the shut door at the end of the hall. "I thought I heard him come in late last night and go into his room."

"He did, but he got up this morning." He leans against the doorframe and crosses his arms. "I heard him stumbling around in *that* bathroom and crying all night, but now I can't find him and I didn't hear him leave. His work called the house, saying he didn't show up, so he's not there."

My fists clench so that my nails dig into my palms. "Did you check in the bathroom?"

Dean's eyes travel down the hall to the bathroom door and he shakes his head. "I haven't and I don't want to."

"Hi, I'm Lila," she introduces herself and offers her hand. "You must be Ella's brother, Dean."

Dean is vaguely amused and shakes her hand. "Yeah… how do you know Ella?"

"I was her roommate," she responds, pressing her hand to her chest, faking being offended. "Didn't she ever mention me?"

"We don't talk that much." I eye the bathroom door again and my stomach twists. "We need to find Dad."

"I'm not looking in that bathroom, Ella, but if you want to, go ahead."

With legs flimsier than wet noodles, I walk down the dark hallway and stop in front of the door, having a flashback of the day my mom died. The door was closed and the house was soundless, except for the running of water. My hands tremble as I open the door.

The room is bare, the tub empty, and the tile floor is clean, except for a small stain. There are no towels on the hooks and the mirror on the wall across from me shows my reflection. My auburn hair is curled perfectly in place, my lips are lined with gloss, and my green eyes are immense and reveal everything.

"Dad isn't in here," I tell him, unable to look away from the mirror. "Are you sure you didn't hear him leave the house?"

"He could have left and I just didn't hear him," he answers. "But when has he ever left the house quietly before?"

I quickly slam the bathroom door, like I'm trying to put out a fire, and race back down the hall. "Someone needs to find him. Did you try and call him?"

"Of course. I'm not a moron." He rolls his eyes and nods. "And he didn't answer."

Lila shifts her weight and forces the uncomfortable conversation elsewhere. "So you play the drums, Dean?"

He motions to his drum set in the middle of his small room with dark blue walls. The floor and bed are cluttered with boxes and the curtain is pulled back, letting the sunlight spill in. "I used to, but I don't much anymore. I have work and a fiancé."

"Fiancé?" Lila and I say simultaneously.

"Yeah, as in we're engaged." Dean rolls his eyes and goes back into his room. "It's what happens when two people date for a really long time."

"Why didn't you tell me?" I ask, following him into his room.

He picks up a small box and drops it onto the floor. "Do you really care that I am?"

I carefully nudge the box out of the way with my foot. "You're my brother. Of course I care."

"But it's not like we've ever really gotten along," he points out. "I haven't even talked to you for a year. God, I didn't even know you went to college until a week ago."

172

He's right, which is sad. I barely know him, he barely knows me, and I'm starting to think I barely know me, too.

"Does Dad know you're engaged?" I ask. "Were you at least planning on telling him?"

"Even if I told him, he'd just forget the next day." He empties a dresser drawer into a large open box and then aligns the drawer back into place. "You know how he is. Christ, I don't even think half the time he knows that you and I don't live here anymore."

"He still deserves to be told," I say. "He's not a bad guy and you know it. He just has problems."

"Problems that fucked up our childhood." He kicks a box out of the way with force and it crashes into the wall. "You do realize that how we grew up wasn't normal. God, even Micha had it easier and his dad bailed out on him, but at least he had a stable mom to take care of him."

"Umm…" Lila pokes her head in the room. "I think I'm going to wait outside for you, Ella."

God, I'd forgotten she was even there and she just heard all of that.

"Okay, I'll be down in a second," I tell her and she leaves readily. I wander around Dean's room, taking in the photos he has up. "I think we may have just scared her to death."

Dean picks up his drumsticks and places them into a large duffel bag. "Okay, I have to ask. How did you end up being friends with her?"

"She was my roommate and we just sort of bonded." I shrug, picking up a photo of Dean and his friends on a sunny beach. It was taken during his Senior Field Trip and he looks happy.

"You bonded," he accuses. "The girl looks like a spoiled princess."

I eye his preppy clothes. "So do you."

"First off, I'm not a princess and I've earned what I have," he says. "It wasn't just handed to me."

"Maybe she did, too."

"Did she?"

I hate to give him the benefit of being right. "No, her parents are pretty well off."

He looks at me with that stupid arrogant expression he gets when I admit he's right. "Well, there you have it then."

"She's nice," I protest. "And she doesn't ask a lot of questions."

"It may seem like you need to keep things to yourself," he says, putting a blanket into a box. "But it's not healthy. You need to find someone you can let it all out to. Otherwise you're going to lose it."

My eyes roam to the window where the edge of Micha's house is visible. "I think I already did."

Dean's forehead creases as he drops a handful of guitar picks into a trunk. "Lose it? Or talk to someone about it?"

"Both." I back toward the door. "When are you heading back to Chicago?"

"Hopefully by tonight. No offense or anything, but this place brings back way too many unpleasant memories."

"Try to say good-bye before you leave."

He doesn't respond and I don't wait around for an answer. That was probably the longest conversation that we've ever had and I have a feeling it may be our last for a very long time.

Chapter 12

Micha

"Dude, where the fuck is your head today?" Ethan asks and seconds later a grease rag hits me in the face.

I throw it back at him, hard. "You're starting to piss me off with this crap."

Ethan widens his eyes exaggeratedly. "Whatever man. You've been so distracted for the last two days." He sticks his head back under the hood. "And I'm not going to say why."

"Good, because I don't want to hear it." I round the back of my car and eye over the tools on the wall of the garage. I grab a rusty toolbox, one of the few things my dad left behind, and toss it into the garbage can. He called again this morning, begging on the answering machine for either my mom or I to pick up.

Ethan raises his head up and eyes the garbage can. "Wanna explain what that was for?"

"Nope." I pick up a wrench and start working on the car.

We work on it for a while, but it's hot and I'm getting more pissed off at my dad by the second. Finally, I move back and throw the wrench down onto the concrete. Ethan doesn't ask questions this time.

"We should have a party tonight," I announce, unable to hold still. "A big one, like the one we had on graduation night."

"You really want to relive that night?" Ethan backs out from under the hood. "Because I'm not sure I do."

I step outside into the sunlight, determined to get my mind off stuff. "What you can't remember doesn't hurt, right?"

"I don't think you want to go there." Ethan walks next to me and we stare down the driveway at an old guy pushing a shopping cart. "There are plenty of times in my life I wish I could remember—that I'd give anything to remember—but I can't. I lost like a year of my life. It's better to stay within the boundaries of a semi-clear head. Besides, this doesn't sound like you at all. What's up?"

"Nothing's up." I sigh, raking my fingers through my hair. "I'm just thinking out loud."

Ethan returns to the garage and starts working on the engine again. Around sophomore year, he started hanging out with these kids at school, who had really heavy views on the world and liked to sit around and get high while they talked about it. Ethan somehow ended up being friends with them, and within a month, he had dropped out of school and got into some pretty heavy shit.

A year later he made the decision to get some help. He cleaned up his life, cut the habits, and worked the hell out of himself to catch up in school. He was a grade behind, but managed to graduate with our year. Looking at him, you wouldn't guess.

The side door of Ella's house swings open and Lila steps out. She looks upset, although not as bad as she did last night. She glances up the driveway at the house across the street, where there's a very loud game of tackle football going on in the front yard. Her eyes roam to my house and then widen when she sees that I'm watching her.

She gives a tentative wave from the top step. "Hey, Micha."

"What's up?" I say with a nod of my chin. "Is Ella up yet?"

Shielding her blue eyes from the sun, she looks up at Ella's window. "Yeah, she said she'd be out in a second. She's just talking to her brother."

"He's not being a dick, is he?"

"I'm not sure what constitutes as a brother being a dick, since I don't have one." A smile cracks at her lips.

I walk toward the fence, pulling up my jeans that are riding low on my hips. "There's no yelling going on?"

Lila shakes her head and meets me at the fence, plucking some of her blonde hair away from her mouth. "But Ella's not much of a yeller, is she?"

I rest my arms on the top of the fence. "It depends on which one we're talking about."

Her face falls. "How could I know her for eight freaking months and not know anything about her. It must say something about me, right?"

I feel bad for her. "I think Ella kind of made it her mission to keep who she was hidden from you. It's not your fault."

She eyes me over with this suspicious look. "Honestly, it seems like she's that way with everyone, except for you."

"We've known each other forever," I say. "We have a comfortable relationship."

Her blue eyes twinkle with mischievousness. "One where you feel her up in the car?"

"It feels like you're trying to start some trouble," I say, liking the girl even more.

"Maybe I am." She leans over the fence to the side of me so she can get a better view of the inside of the garage. "Is that Ethan in there?"

I step back so she can get a better look. "Yep, he's working on the car."

"I think I'll go give him some help." A grin spans across her face and she hops over the fence, squealing as her shoe gets caught in the wire.

Trying not to laugh at her, I unhook her shoe and she walks into the garage, surprising Ethan. The door to Ella's house opens and my attention centers on her as she steps out into the sunlight.

She's wearing a tight, black and purple plaid dress, and knee high lace-up boots, but her hair is curled up neatly. It's like a mix of her old look and her new one. Her face is guarded as she ambles across the driveway, with this strange look in her eyes, like she's terrified yet excited at the same time.

"Did Lila come out here?" She bites her lip and I want to lean over and bite it for her; taste her and feel her like I did last night.

Without taking my eyes off her, I nod my head at the garage. "She's in there with Ethan. I think she might have a thing for him."

"I think you're right." She pauses. "I think I might have freaked her out a little, just barely."

"You mean you and Dean might have freaked her out a little?"

"She told you I was talking to Dean?"

"She mentioned it." I extend my hand to her. "Why don't you come over and join the party on this side of the fence?"

"A party of four?" she asks, trying not to grin and looking as cute as hell.

I snag her by the hip, jerk her toward me playfully, and dip my lips to her ear. "It can be a party of two. Just say the word."

She shivers from the feel of my breath on her neck. "I think we better keep it a foursome."

I press my fingers into the curve of her hips. "I didn't know you liked it kinky."

She swats my shoulder and I laugh, my dad problems feeling less heavy. "Relax, I was just kidding, even though you're the one who brought it up first."

"I was joking."

"I know... I think I am going to have a party tonight."

"Don't you have one of those every night?"

I cock my eyebrow. "Besides the night you showed up, have you seen one going on?"

She wrinkles her forehead. "No." She sits down on the fence, swinging her legs over to my side. "Micha, what have you been doing for the last eight months?"

"Pinning for you." I avoid the truth. That I haven't been doing much of anything besides looking for her and helping my mom take care of things.

She tucks her dress underneath her legs and I get a small glimpse of the black lacy panties she has on. "Where do you work?"

Against her protest, I spread her legs apart and put myself between them. "I work at the shop with Ethan a lot, but it's not going to be forever. I have plans. I'm still working on getting everything lined up."

She places her hands on my chest, holding me back. "I think the lines between our friendship are getting a little blurred."

"That happened a long time ago," I tell her, gliding my palms up the sides of her bare legs. "At least for me it did."

Her jaw tightens. "It's things like that that which make them blurry and things last night… and things like in the car."

"There seems to be a lot of things, which I think might be a hint that you and I belong together."

Her eyes snap wide and I back off to try another tactic. She needs to smile and let those stressed lips free. I pinch her side and she squeals.

"Don't do that," she says, holding back a laugh. "You know I hate being tickled."

I graze my fingers across her other side and she squirms, before falling over the fence and landing on her back in the grass. I leap over the fence easily as she scrambles to her feet. She narrows her eyes, backing toward her back door. I run up to the side of her and she skitters out of my reach. She glances at the door and then at the front yard, which is closer to her.

"Micha, seriously," she warns. "We're too old for this."

I spread my arms out to the side innocently. "I'm not doing anything."

Her eyes flick to her house one last time and then shaking her head, she spins around and runs for the front yard. I give her a head start before I sprint off after her. When I round the house, she's up on the front porch, jiggling the door knob.

I laugh at her. "Is it locked?"

She heaves a frustrated sigh and hops over the railing, slipping on the grass. "Dammit Micha! I'm so going to kick your ass for this."

"I'm planning on holding you to that threat." I jog after her across the neighbor's yard.

She races across the grass, her hair falling out of a clip. She leaps over the brick fence into the next yard and smashes a row of flowers. Without using my hands, I hop onto the fence, but trip during my dismount and fall on my knees.

She freezes in the middle of the lawn and starts to laugh at me. "You so deserved that."

I get to my feet, dusting the dirt off my knees, and a dark smile rises on my face. "You think that's funny?"

Her eyes sparkle and it's worth the fall. "You look ridiculous."

"Do I?" I take a step toward her.

She takes a step back. "You do."

Abruptly the sprinklers turn on, drenching the grass and her. She screams and covers her head with her arms.

"Serves you right for laughing at me," I say with a grin.

She lets her arms fall to the side and smirks. "Well, at least it keeps you away from me."

Her dress is clinging to her body in all the right places and pieces of her wet hair stick to the sides of her face. She begins to twirl in circles with her hands up above her head.

"You're beautiful," I say, unable to help myself.

Ella

Micha looks ridiculous and I can't help but laugh. I haven't laughed in so long that it feels unnatural leaving my mouth. It's like we're kids again, as if this moment belongs in another time where things are weightless and full of sunshine.

As I'm laughing at him, the sprinklers turn on and my clothes instantly get soaked. At first I squeal, but then I let go, lifting my hands above my head and twirling in the water, figuring he won't come in after me.

He calls out something about me being beautiful and then he charges into the sprinklers, completely blind-siding me. His arms snake around my waist and we collapse to the ground but Micha holds my weight up, so I land on the wet grass gently.

"Micha," I say, trying to be serious. "Don't do it. You know how much I hate being tickled."

"Which makes it even more appealing." Water beads in his hair, his long eyelashes, his lips. With one hand, he pins my arms above my head and presses his body against mine. My wet clothes cling to my skin and I can feel every part of him. "I take that back. This is more appealing." He lets his hand move up my ribs, his thumb sketching along the ridges, sending my body into a frenzy.

I stop fighting him and lay perfectly still. Water sprinkles our faces as he lowers his lips to mine. Our wet tongues twine together, full of desire as they collide. A strange, unfamiliar feeling opens inside of me again and my legs fall apart and hook around his waist, requesting more of him, like they did last night.

Micha draws back, looking surprised as he glances at the house to the side of us and then at the street. Then he lets out an untamed growl and deepens the kiss, thrusting his tongue deep into my mouth. I suck on his bottom lip and trace my tongue along his lip ring. It sends a quiver through his body and I'm secretly pleased, but my pleasure confuses me.

"Ella," he groans and then kisses me fiercely. His hand travels upward and cups my breasts. His thumb circles around my nipple and through the wet fabric of my clothes, the feeling is mind blowing. It's driving me wild and my knees vice-grip against his hips.

A moan laced with ecstasy crumbles from my lips. I'm starting to lose control again and it's alarming. I try to get past it this time, but it consumes me and I have to stop. After a lot of effort, I get my arms between our bodies and I push him away.

"We should get back." I look at the brick home of the yard we're laying in. "Besides if Miss Fenerly comes out, she'll have a heart attack."

Micha's aqua eyes penetrate me. There's mud on his forehead and grass in the locks of his blonde hair. "If that's what you want." Maneuvering to his feet, he takes my hand and lifts me to mine. He plucks pieces of grass out of my hair and lets his hand linger on my cheek.

Holding hands, we walk across the grass and down the sidewalk, leaving a trail of water behind us and something else. Something invisible to the outside eye, but to me it's more noticeable than the sun in the sky.

Chapter 13

Micha

I'm determined to have a party tonight, even though I'm
not a fan of parties. Never really have been. I just like how
they block out all the noise inside my head and what I'm
hoping is that tonight's will block out the sound of my
dad's voice.

Ella bailed on me when we got back to our houses,
muttering something about finding her father. I offered to
go with her, but she declined and took Lila instead. I let
her be because I sensed she needed space. I was fine with
her taking some time as long as it wasn't the space of five
hundred miles.

Ethan and I take a break from working on the car to
plan the party. After a massive amount of text messages
are sent out and a couple of keggers ordered by Ethan,
we're good to go.

We're hanging around in the kitchen, waiting for people to start showing up when clouds start rolling in and thunder rattles at the windows.

"Can I ask you something?" Ethan asks abruptly.

I take out a frozen burrito from the freezer and drop it on a plate. "Sure. What's up?"

"Don't take this the wrong way." He tips back in his chair. "But what is it with Ella? Why are you so fixated on her? You have like a ton of girls falling at your feet all the time and you used to totally be all into it. Then suddenly you weren't and it was all about her."

"I wasn't ever into the girls falling at my feet. I was just bored." I pop the plate into the microwave and press start.

He grabs a handful of chips from a bag on the table. "Okay, but that still doesn't answer my question."

I cross my arms, uncomfortable with the awkward heart-to-heart moment. "I'm not sure, but why do you care?"

"I'm just curious because you've never talked about it."

"Yeah, but we don't talk about a lot of stuff."

He lets the chair legs reconnect to the floor. "Look, I'm not asking you to open up and spill your feelings out to me, so quit being weird. I just want to understand because I've known both of you practically forever."

The microwave beeps and I turn to it. "It was the night of the snowboarding incident. That's when I realized things were different."

"When she broke her arm?" he asks. "And you had to take her to the hospital."

I nod. "You remember how she fell off the roof and then didn't get up right away and certain *people* were yelling that she was dead."

"Hey, I was drunk," Ethan gripes because he was the one yelling. "And she looked dead to me."

"Well, that's when I knew." I take the burrito out and set it on the counter. "Thinking she was dead was seriously the most terrifying thing that's ever happened to me. More than the idea of my father never returning. More than my own death."

Ethan nods, trying to make sense of my babbling. "Okay..."

I slam the microwave door shut and sit down at the table. "Hey, you asked."

He taps his phone on the table. "What do you think of Lila?"

"She seems nice." I get up and grab a soda from the fridge and then toss one to Ethan. "And she seems to be into you, I guess."

He taps the top of the can, and then flips the tab. "Yeah, but she barely knows me."

Sipping my soda, I sit back down. "Everyone barely knows you."

He shrugs, staring out the window. "I never really understood the point of that whole get-to-know-you thing."

The house phone rings and our conversation ends. I inhale the rest of the burrito as the answer machine beeps.

"Um, hi... this message is for Micha." It's my father's voice.

I freeze, gripping the edge of the table.

"Look, Terri, I understand that he's pissed at me, but I need to talk to him. It's important, okay? And he hung up on me yesterday morning... I thought maybe if you encouraged him to call me?" He sounds frazzled. "I don't know... look, I'm sorry." He hangs up.

I release the table from my death grip, get up, and delete the message from the phone. When I turn around, Ethan is on his feet. The hole that I punched in the wall hasn't been fixed and I think about hammering my fist through it again.

"We should get our shit picked up before it rains," Ethan says, staring at the sky through the window.

I pop my knuckles and walk for the door. "Sounds like a plan."

Ella

I find my dad at the bar. It's the first place I look, but it's disappointing that it was so easy. Lila waits for me in the car, because I ask her to. When I walk in, I spot him slumped over in a barstool with an empty cup in front of him. Denny, the bartender, is wiping down the counters with a rag. When he sees me in the entryway, he holds up his hand.

"You're going to need to show me your ID, before you come in any further." He drapes the cleaning rag over his shoulder and walks around the counter toward me.

"It's me, Denny," I say. "Ella Daniels."

His eyes widen. "Holy shit. You're back."

I nod. "I am, but only for the summer."

He rakes his hands through his curly brown hair. "Where were you anyway? No one really seemed to know."

"In Las Vegas, going to school." I point at my father. "I should probably take him home, I'm guessing."

Denny glances back at my father. "He stumbled in here early this morning. I wasn't even opened up yet, but he was already too drunk to understand when I tried to explain to him that we were closed."

"I'll take him home," I tell him and he lets me by. "I'm sorry he's been so much trouble for you."

192

He drops the rag on the counter and helps me get my dad to his feet. He smells like he showered in a bottle of Jack Daniels.

"I don't mind him being here, Ella," Denny says. "But I'm starting to feel guilty about it. For the last few months, he's been showing up more and more. I think he might have a problem."

"He's had one for a while." I drape my dad's arm over my shoulder and Denny does the same with his other arm.

My dad mumbles an incoherent objection and then something about missing her and wanting it to all go away. We drag him outside and Lila hops out of the car. She doesn't say anything as Denny and I lie my dad down in the back of the Firebird.

It's starting to sprinkle and lightning snaps across the sky.

"Thanks for helping me get him out," I tell Denny, shielding my eyes from the raindrops.

Denny rubs his neck tensely. "Have you ever considered getting him some help?"

"What do you mean? Like rehab?" I shout over the thunder.

He shrugs. "Or AA. Something that will help him get his life together."

I scratch my head, confused. Why hadn't it occurred to me? Panic starts to claw up my throat and guilty feelings about my mother's death consume me.

"Just think about it," Denny says, giving me a pat on the arm. "And if you need any help, you know where to find me."

I thank him again and jump into the car. I wait for Lila to say something, but when she opens her mouth, it's not what I was expecting.

"My older sister was a drug addict," she says quickly. "For like a year."

I stop chewing on my gum. "I didn't know that."

"I know. Not a lot of people do. My family is very firm on keeping our dirty laundry to ourselves." She rotates in her chair to look at my dad snoring on the backseat. "But I wanted to tell you so that you know that I understand how hard it is to watch someone you care about hurt themselves."

I turn the car down my street and the tires splash puddles onto the hood as they hit the potholes. "Why did you never tell me before?"

"Why didn't you tell me about your dad?"

"I don't know." Who is this girl sitting next to me? "So my life doesn't scare you?"

She arches her eyebrows and sits forward in her seat. "I wouldn't go that far, but your personal life doesn't."

194

Jessica Sorensen

***

There are three large Keggers on Micha's back porch when
we pull up to my house. The garage door is wide open and
his car is missing. The rain is pouring down and flooding
the sidewalk and the tree next to the house sways in the
wind.

"They must have got the car fixed," I say, unbuckling
my seatbelt.

"Dang it." Lila smacks her hand on her knee and a
smile expands across her face. "I was so looking forward
to watching Ethan bent over the hood."

I snort a laugh. "Well, that wasn't really my point," I
say when I stop laughing. "We somehow have to get him
out of the car and into the house and I was going to have
Micha help."

Lila and I turn toward the backseat, trying to figure
out a way to get my dad out.

"Maybe we could ask your brother?" Lila suggests.

My eyes roam to the Porsche parked in front of us.
"I'm not sure he'll help even if we ask him."

"It doesn't hurt to try."

"Yeah, you're right." I sigh and text Dean to come
help. He doesn't answer, but a few minutes later the back
door swings open. Dean steps out, barefoot, with a hoodie
pulled over his head. He doesn't say anything when he
swings the door open. Lila hops out of his way and he

195

ducks inside the car and drags our father out. I scramble out of the car and hold the back door open for him. He lets my dad lean his weight on him and he aides him to the living room sofa.

"Where did you find him?" Dean asks me as he turns my dad to his side in case he throws up.

"At the bar." I place the duvet from the back of the couch over my dad and he snuggles up to it like a child. "Denny helped me get him to the car."

Dean presses his lips together, and bobs his head up and down. "That's where I figured he was, but I didn't want to go looking for him."

"You know I'm not even old enough to be in a bar, right?"

"And I'm old enough to know that I don't want to deal with this crap anymore."

I open my mouth to yell at him but zip my lips and shake my head, regaining power of my temper.

He backs toward the stairway. "I've had enough. I'm moving on with my life and you should do the same." He leaves me in the room alone with a heavy feeling in my heart.

I'd love to move on, but I'm not sure how. Running away to Vegas for eight months sure as hell didn't help because I'm almost back to where I started.

***

Lila and I decide to go to Larry's Diner, the local fast food drive-in, to get some lunch. It's a seventies themed restaurant where the waitresses wear roller skates and skate up the cars to take orders. After they hook the food tray to the window, we eat in the car and listen to music.

The rain is still beating down, but softer, although the roof is draining onto the front of the hood. We're chatting about the group of guys sitting on the tables underneath the canopy, when Lila focuses the conversation to somewhere I don't want to go.

"So where did you and Micha run off to this morning?" she asks, sipping her soda and batting her eyelashes innocently.

I dip a fry in the ranch cup balanced on the console. "Nowhere. He just chased me down the street."

She dumps some more ketchup onto her chicken sandwich. "Then why did both of you come back soaking wet?"

My body tingles at the memory of Micha and me rolling around in the grass. "One of the neighbor's sprinklers turned on while we were running across it."

"Seems like you were awfully wet just from being in the sprinklers for a few minutes." She dabs her lips with a napkin. "And you look really happy right now."

I force back a smile and pick the pickles off my burger silently.

"If you don't want to tell me," she says. "Then you don't have to."

"I'm just not comfortable talking about Micha," I explain. "When I don't even know how I feel about him."

"Okay, well you could talk to me about it. That's how friends help each other figure things out." She pauses, cleaning up some grease that dripped on her shirt. "Didn't you ever have a friend that you could talk to about everything?"

I shrug and take a bite of my burger. "Micha maybe, but I can't talk to him about him."

She looks at me sadly. "Try talking to me then."

I chew on a fry, trying not to choke. Once it's out there, it's real. "I'm not sure I can."

"Just try," she urges. "What's it going to hurt?"

I stir the ranch with a fry. "Micha kissed me on the front lawn. That's why we came back all wet. We were lying on the grass, getting soaked by the sprinklers and making out."

"Did you like it?"

"Like what?"

She rolls her eyes. "The kiss."

"I like it every time he kisses me," I say nonchalantly. "Yet at the same time, I don't. My feelings are conflicted."

"Because you don't know what you want?" she asks.

"No, I think I do know what I want," I mumble, stunned by my own answer. "I just won't admit it."

She says, "I think you just did."

I continue thinking out loud. "I think I might have figured it out that night on the bridge..." My mind starts to drift back to that night as I stare at the rain pattering against the windshield.

She slurps her soda. "What happened the night on the bridge?"

"I kissed Micha." I shut my eyes, drifting back to the memory, not on the bridge but somewhere else we went that night. We're in his car talking. He seems happy and so do I.

She giggles. "I knew it. I knew he wasn't just a friend. So tell me the details, like what happened after the kiss."

My eyes open to a veil of rain on the window as the images drift away from my mind. "Nothing. I left for college."

She balls up the sandwich wrapper and sets it in the bag. "You just *left*? God, no wonder you two visually undress each other. The sexual tension between you is probably about ready to burst."

I start to deny it, but realize she's right. I want Micha so badly it physically hurts sometimes, however if it hurts to want him this much, then how bad would it be to lose him?

"Speaking of the devil." She rolls down the window as Micha's Chevelle pulls up beside us. "What are you like stalking us or something?"

Ethan leans over from the passenger side and hollers, "How did you ever guess?"

Micha's extremely quiet, as he reads the menu on the marquee. The waitress skates over and ducks her head into the cab of the car, sticking out her butt. Rain falls on her back as she jots down their orders and then giggles at something either Micha or Ethan said. Either way, it's annoying. I pile all the garbage onto the tray, start up the car, and rev up the engine, startling the waitress and everyone else.

Lila gapes at me. "Ella, what are you doing?"

"Sorry," I apologize, feeling kind of bad, and put a tip on the tray. The waitress gives me a tight smile as she collects the tray and skates off to the order window.

Micha hops out of the car and his boots splash in the puddles. He stretches his long legs and arms, and then winds around the back of my car and to my door. He taps his fist on the window. Sighing, I roll it down.

He crouches down so we're eyelevel and rests his arms on the seal of the window. "Do you want to explain what that was about?"

"An accidental slip of the foot," I say, knowing he's going to read straight through my bull shit lie. "Sometimes it happens."

"Not with you." His eyes twinkle like sapphires as raindrops bead down his face. "If you want my attention, just say so."

"I want your attention." The truth falls from my lips, shocking us both.

He kisses me on the forehead with his wet lips. "See, that wasn't so hard."

"Yes, it was," I surrender, defeated. "But I'm tired."

"Of being someone you're not?"

"That among other things."

He lets out an unsteady breath and lowers his voice as he leans close to my ear. "Are you ready to talk about it?"

I shake my head. "Not yet, but maybe soon."

"I'm here when you're ready." He gives a soft suck on the sensitive spot right below my ear, and his tongue tastes my skin before he pulls away.

"You want to race home?" He wiggles his eyebrows, teasing me. "Loser owes the other one a favor."

I scrunch up my nose and glance over at his Chevelle. "I'm not stupid enough to think I could ever win that bet."

He laughs, sucking his lip ring into his mouth. "I promise I'll go easy on you."

A naughty feeling dances inside me. "What if I don't want you to go easy on me?"

He's speechless, which is rare. His gaze bores into me and then he strides forward and kisses me. It's quick, but it steals my breath away.

Chapter 14

Micha

We end up racing home. I let her win, even though I'd love to have the favor, which would include lots of dirty things that she's not ready for. So now I owe her a favor and she tells me she has to think about it, with this little tease in her voice that makes me grin.

We part ways at our houses and she leaves me with the promise she'll try to come over later tonight. She's slowly changing back into the girl I know, although that night still haunts her eyes, but I'm not sure she'll ever really get over it completely.

It's still raining and lightning like hell, which means the party's going to have to take place inside. Ethan and I drag the wet keggers inside and stand them on the kitchen table. There's a note tacked on the wall from my mom, telling me she's going to be home late.

Ethan starts rummaging through the cupboards for some food. "What band's playing?"

"Naomi's." I head to my room to change and get my guitar. "Answer the door if anyone knocks."

In my room, I tug on a grey t-shirt and pull a black pin-striped shirt over it. I slip on a pair of black jeans and put on a studded belt. Then I grab my guitar and text Naomi.

Me: When u planning on heading over?"

Naomi: Soon. Why? You waiting on us to tell us some super exciting news.

Me: I haven't decided yet.

Naomi: Don't turn it down. It's a great opportunity.

Me: I'm not sayin yes or no. See u in a bit.

When Naomi took me backstage at the coffeehouse, she first proposed the idea that I should replace their guitarist and hit the road with them. At first, I was all for it. It's what I've wanted to do since I was twelve and rocked out with Ethan and Dean in the garage. But then I thought back to Ella's sad eyes and doubts washed over me.

The doorbell rings and I head to the living room to get the party started and clear my head for one night.

Ella

By the time I decide to go over to Micha's, things are already getting out of hand. Cars are parked on the lawn, and garbage cans are tipped over. Someone's even sitting on the roof.

Lila talks me into going and we run up the driveway with our arms over our heads to shield our hair from the rain, but the crowded foyer overwhelms me and I start to back out.

"Stop being a baby and go in there," she says, giving me a gentle shove forward. "I want to see the tough girl everyone keeps talking about."

"No, you don't. Trust me," I tell her. "She was mean and she would have never been friends with you."

"Okay, then show me a happy medium." She has a dark blue, strapless dress on that matches her shoes and her blonde hair rests on her shoulders in curls, which have slipped loose because of the rain. "You can change yourself without losing your identity completely."

I turn away from the crowd toward her. "Why have we never talked like this before?"

She smiles sadly. "Because you would never let us."

She says something else, but the music stifles her words. I fan the smoke from my face and step into the kitchen. Holding the bottom of my black skirt, I maneuver through the crowd toward the table. I lose Lila for a moment, but when the crowd thins, Lila stumbles out, stomping on a guy's foot with her high heel.

She curses, fussing with her hair. "Has Micha ever heard of a little thing called air conditioning?"

"He probably forgot to turn it on!" I shout over the music. "Wait here. I'll go turn it up."

I squeeze through the crowd toward the living room and the band. The music is deafening and I realize it's Micha playing with Naomi. They're sharing the microphone and he looks like he's enjoying himself. I stop in the middle of the room and watch him from the crowd. He's gorgeous under the light with his hair hanging in his eyes as he spills out his lyrics to people and strums on the guitar.

I back through the room and into the hall. There's a couple making out in front of the thermostat. The music quiets down and then starts up again as I gently guide them over and they move out of my way without breaking their lips from each other. Fanning my face, I turn up the cold air. Suddenly, long arms encircle my waist and the scent of him fills my chest.

"I thought you were playing," I yell over the music with my hand pressed to my heart.

"I was, but I took a break to see you." His breath smells like beer.

I scrunch up my nose. "Are you drunk?"

"I've only had one beer," he says. "I'm just excited to see you."

"And to be playing again," I state.

His smile is huge and it makes me happy for a moment. "Yeah, that too. I saw you watching me."

I shrug, playing it off. "I'm glad you're happy. You looked sad earlier at the drive-in."

His hand finds my hip and he grips it tightly, sending heat through my body. "I'm even happier now that you're here."

I relax against the wall. "You know I've heard you use that pickup line on girls before, right?"

"Come on, let me have some fun with you," he begs with a tease in his voice. "Pretend like you don't know any of my moves."

"You want me to pretend like I'm someone else?" I question. "Haven't you been telling me to do the opposite?"

The reflection of the light dances in his eyes as he leans forward and wisps of his hair brush my cheek. "Just be the girl I used to know. The one that had fun and laughed all the time."

"That girl would have never pretended with you, even if you requested her to."

"I know that."

His other hand finds my waist and his body slants toward me. Glancing from left to right, I slide my hands up his firm chest and link them around his neck. Then I pull myself onto him and hitch my legs around his waist. His expression is stoic, but he lets out a growl and his lips come down hard on mine. Our chests press together as he thrusts his body into me. Our tongues connect, feeling each other thoroughly. My back is pressed into the thermostat and my skirt barely covers the top of my thighs. My head falls back against the wall as he trails kisses down my neck. My breathing is rapid and so is my pulse. What is he doing to me?

The music stops and Naomi's voice rises over the speakers. "Micha Scott, get your ass back up here and play right now."

Micha pulls away, breathless. "I have one more song to play and then you and I are going to pick right back up with this."

Before I can answer, he leaves me in the hall. Touching my lips, I watch him weave back to the stage, knowing if he does pick it up, I'm not going to be able to stop it this time. Struggling with the loss of control over my own body, I wander back into the kitchen. Lila's over by the cooler, sipping on a drink and talking to Ethan. Straightening my shoulders, I march up to the counter and pour myself a drink. Lila and Ethan's eyes are on me as I knock it back. The alcohol burns my throat as I slam the cup down on the counter. "Who's up for a game of quarters?"

***

Two hours and three shots later, I'm feeling pretty good. The band has finished playing and Micha has joined our game at the table. "Sail" by *AWOLNATION* beats through the stereo, soft lyrics and a sultry rhythm and it takes me back to another time.

"I think I'm going to go dance," I announce to the table.

"Ah ha, I knew you secretly liked to dance." Lila slams her hand down on the table and then hiccups. "Oh, excuse me."

Ethan laughs at her like she's the cutest thing in the world. "Are you reaching your limit little girl?"

Lila narrows her eyes impishly at Ethan. "I'm not the one who missed the last three shots."

He replies with a comeback, but I don't hear it as I rise from my chair anxious to dance. Micha watches me inquisitively as I make a path through the crowd. Faceless people bead with sweat and the air smells like salt and is lit with desirable heat. The farther I descend into the crowd the hotter it gets. By the time I'm in the center, my skin is damp with sweat and the thin fabric of my strapless shirt is sticking to my back.

There's a darkness inside my chest, like the devil hidden inside me is about to make a grand appearance. I raise my hands and sway my hips, letting my hair fall down my shoulders and back. I breathe freely, just like I use to. The more the music plays, the more relaxed I become. My head falls from side to side and my eyelids drift shut.

I feel someone move up behind me and they smell of desire mingled with an earthy scent and something mouthwatering.

Micha places his hands on my hips, his hands domineering. He nearly melts me as he spreads his fingers around my waist and presses his body against mine, wanting as much of me as he can get.

"I thought you didn't dance anymore," he whispers in a feral voice, his warm breath touching every part of me.

I lean back into him, comfortable, and breathe in his familiar scent. "I guess I'm a liar."

"You didn't use to be." He sweeps my hair to the side and implores our bodies closer as he moves with me. Through the fabric of our clothes, I feel the heat radiating off him like the sun. "In fact, you used to be the most honest person I knew."

I slant my head back against his chest. "I know, and I'm working on getting it back."

"Good, I'm glad." His hands slide down my hips and don't stop until they reach the hem of my skirt. "Weren't you and I supposed to finish what we started in the hall?"

I start to pull away, but he intensifies his embrace and restrains me against him so we're bonded in every way possible. I feel the hardness of his chest and the heat emitting off every single God damn part of him. It makes me want to moan.

"You're fucking driving me crazy. You know that?" He whispers through a groan as his fingers slip underneath the side of my skirt and up my thighs. "I want you, pretty girl. *Badly*." He's not lying. His desire is pressed up against the back of my waist.

I should stop him… He's practically got his hand up my dress and we're surrounded by a ton of people, but I give in to him, subsiding in his arms, and let his fingers inch higher up my skirt. Slowly, he kisses my skin, before parting his lips and nipping my neck, sucking, tasting, driving my body mad. His other hand wanders upward on the outside of my shirt and over the curve of my breast. I practically come undone in his arms. Without warning, I turn around, slipping out of his grip. I secure my arms around his neck. His eyes darken as he welds our bodies back together.

My head falls back, allowing him access as I put my weight into his lean arms. He holds me tightly, tracking kisses down the hollow of my neck, licking my collar bone, delving lower and lower as his hand sneaks for the bottom of my skirt again and the palm of his hand caresses the back of my thigh.

He groans, cupping the back of my head with his other hand, then suddenly he pulls away. "How drunk are you?"

I glance from left to right like there's an answer hidden in the crowd. "I don't know."

He sighs and drags his fingers through his hair. "You're killing me, you know that?"

"I'm sorry." I pout.

He laughs and directs me back over to the table. "Go meet up with Lila and I'll be there in a bit, okay."

"Why? Where are you going?" I ask.

He rubs his hand across his face and lets out a breathy laugh. "I have to go take care of some business."

We part ways and I go back to the kitchen like he told me. Lila's eyes are accusing as I sit down at the table. I try not to smile, but I'm too intoxicated to care.

"Look at you," Lila says. "All smiley."

I start to say something, but spot Micha talking to Naomi in the middle of the crowd. She laughs at something he says and then the two of them head toward the hall where his bedroom is.

I guess that was the business he had to take care of. I get up from the table and without another word I run outside into the rain.

Micha

Ella is killing me tonight. I've got a hard on so bad, it's probably going to take an hour in an ice-cold shower to calm me down and she's drunk, so I can't take it any further. I head back to my room, to take care of the problem myself, when Naomi meets up with me.

She waves her finger at me and then laughs. "You and I need to talk."

"I still haven't decided!" I shout over the music.

She takes me by the arm and tugs me down the hall, bumping people out of the way until we reach my room. She shuts the door and flips on the light. "Alright, please explain to me why it's so hard to make the decision about something you've always wanted to do?"

"I'd rather not."

She throws her hands in the air, exasperatedly. "I don't get you. All you used to talk about in high school was playing in a band on the road."

"I still do," I say. "But I'm not sure if I can leave people behind.

Her face relaxes and her hands fall to her side. "I actually get that. I was worried to leave my dad alone, but I talked to him and explained why and you know what? He understood."

"Mine's more complicated, Naomi." I sit down on the bed, wishing she'd leave. "It's not just my mom I'm worried about."

She sits down on the bed beside me and crosses her legs. "It's because of Ella."

"Fuck, am I that obvious," I say. "Because I always thought I was subtle."

She snorts a laugh. "You've never been subtle. And it's not just you. It's both of you. But you know what, you can't center you're life around one girl. You gotta move on and live life the way you want to."

She doesn't get it. "Yeah, let's not talk about this."

"Alright." She holds her hands up. "Sorry, I'll let you be. I just wanted to give you something to think about."

She pats me on the knee before heading out into the hall. Once the door shuts, I fall back onto my bed. Maybe she's right. Maybe it is time to let go of her.

"Fuck." I need resolution.

My eyes wander toward Ella's house. It is dark, except for one light. The bathroom where her mother died. That light hasn't been on for eight months. Why is it on now?

Chapter 15

8 months earlier…

Ella

"You're not seriously going to climb up that tree, are you?" Micha frowns at me through the dark. He's dressed in a pair of sexy jeans that make his butt look good and his black t-shirt fits him perfectly. "You're gonna break your neck."

I rub my hands together and give him a devious look. "You know how much I love a challenge."

From behind him, the moon shines from the sky and his blonde hair nearly glows. "Yeah, but you're a little out of it right now and I don't think you should be climbing up any trees."

"I'll be fine." I wave him off, pushing the sleeves of my leather jacket up. He always worries about me. I like that he does, but it doesn't mean I always listen to him. "Besides, if my dad catches me coming in, and he happens to be sober, I'm going to get chewed out for sneaking out and being drunk, especially because I was supposed to be on mom duty tonight."

Gripping a branch, I attempt to wedge my foot up in the tree. But it falls to the ground and I grunt with frustration. Micha laughs, shaking his head as he walks around behind me.

"If you break your neck, pretty girl," he says. "It's not my fault."

"You know your nickname for me is not fitting." I grab the branch again. "You need to think of a new one."

He sweeps my hair to the side and puts his lips beside my ear. "It's completely fitting. You're the most beautiful girl I know, Ella May."

Through my foggy brain, I try to process what he's saying. "Are you trying to be funny?"

He shakes his head. "I'm being completely serious. But there's no need to panic. I'm sure you'll forget all about it by the time morning rolls around."

I bob my head up and down. "You're probably right."

He laughs again and his warm breath tickles my ear, sending a shiver through my body. I almost turn around, rip open his shirt, and thrust my tongue into his mouth, but I don't want to ruin our friendship. He's all I have at the moment and I need him more than air. So I bottle my feelings up the best I can.

He spreads his fingers across my waist where my shirt rides up, making the situation a little awkward. "Okay, on the count of three I'm going to boost you into the tree. *Be Careful*. One… Two… Three…" He lifts me up into the tree and I swing my legs up. The bark scratches at the back of my legs a little and the palms of Micha's hands cup my ass as he pushes me up the rest of the way. It makes me giggle.

Once I'm up, he climbs up himself. His hands reunite with my waist and he assists me up the tree and into my window. I tumble through it and onto the floor with his quiet laughter surrounding me.

"You're going to regret this in the morning," he says with laughter in his voice. "You're going to have a headache from hell."

I kneel beside the window as he steps back out onto the branch. "Hey, Micha." I crook my finger at him and he rolls his eyes, but tolerates me and returns to the windowsill. I throw my arms around his neck. "You're my hero. You know that?" I kiss his cheek. His skin is so soft. I start to move away when his head turns toward me and our lips connect briefly. When he pulls back, I can't read him at all.

"Sweet dreams, pretty girl." He grins and climbs back down the tree.

My head becomes even foggier as I shut the window. Did he kiss me on purpose? I shake the thought away and wrestle my arms out of my jacket. The house is silent, except for the sound of flowing water coming from the bathroom. I head out into the hall, figuring my mom's left the bath running again. She does that sometimes when she's distracted. The door is locked, so I knock on it.

"Mom, are you in there?" I call out.

Water swishes from inside and I realize the carpet beneath my feet is sloshy. I sober up real quick, and rush to my closet to grab a hanger. Stretching it out, I shove the end into the lock of the bathroom. It clicks and I push the door open.

The scream that leaves my mouth could shatter the world's happiness into a thousand pieces. But the silence that follows it is enough to dissolve it completely.

Micha

"What are you so happy about tonight?" my mom questions when I walk into the house.

"I'm as happy as I always am." I join her at the kitchen table and steal a cookie from a plate.

She takes off her glasses and rubs the sides of her nose. There's a calculator, a checkbook, and a whole lot of bills stacked in front of her. "No, I haven't seen you smile like this in a while."

"I just had a really good night." I take out my wallet and hand my mom a couple of twenties and a hundred dollar bill. "Here, this is what I got for working a weekend at the shop."

My mom shakes her head and tosses the money in my direction. "Micha Scott, I'm not going to take my son's money."

I throw it on top of the bills and push away from the table. "Yes, you are. I want to help out."

"Micha I—"

"Stop arguing and take it young lady," I warn with humor in my tone.

She sighs, defeated, and collects the money. "You're a good son. Do you know that?"

"Only because I was taught to be." I head for my room, but hear a scream from outside. I backtrack into the kitchen. "Did you just hear that?"

My mom's eyes are wide as she stares at the back door. "I think it came from the Daniel's house."

A billion different scenarios rush through my head as I run outside, hop the fence, and burst into her house. "El-la!"

It's quiet, except for water running upstairs. I dash up the staircase, skipping steps. "Ella..." My body chills like ice. Ella is standing in the doorway and her mom is in the bathtub filled with red water that's spilling out all over the floor. "Ella, what happened?"

She flinches and then turns to me. Her pupils have taken over her eyes and the look on her face will haunt me for the rest of my life.

"I think she killed herself," she says numbly and holds out her hands, which are smudged with blood. "I checked her pulse and she doesn't have one."

I take out my cell phone and call 911. When I hang up, Ella collapses into my arms and stays there, unmoving until the ambulance shows up. She doesn't cry—she barely breathes and it nearly kills me because I can't do anything to help her.

Chapter 16

Current Day

Ella

I don't know why I'm in here. I started to run down the street with so much adrenaline lashing through me it felt like my chest was going to explode. The rain was pouring down and all I could think about was getting as far away from Micha's house as possible, but my mind caught up with me and I pulled myself back somehow.

My clothes drip on the bathroom floor, which is still stained red from her blood. I sit down and hug my knees to my chest, staring at the bathtub.

Something died in me when I found her, but I'm not sure what. Maybe my soul. That night, I'd been so determined to go to that stupid party that I left her at the house alone, even though my dad had left me in charge of her.

There was one simple rule: keep an eye on mom. And I couldn't even follow it.

"Ella, what are you doing in here?" Micha observes me from the doorway, his clothes and hair drenched with rain.

I cuddle my knees against me and squeeze my eyes shut. "I saw you go to your bedroom with Naomi."

"Okay…" he sounds confused. "Why do you sound upset, though?"

"It doesn't matter," I say. "None of this matters."

"Of course it matters." He sits down beside me and drapes his arm over his knees. "Otherwise you wouldn't be in here."

"You're right, it does matter." I run my finger between the cracks in the tile. "I don't want you to be with Naomi."

"Wait a minute. Do you think I hooked up with her?"

"Isn't that what you normally do when you take a girl back to your room?"

"Naomi and I were just talking," he mutters quietly. "And I haven't *taken* a girl back to my room in months."

Hearing him say that makes me feel better and I start to face the inevitable. I can run all I want and try to shut myself down, but my feelings for Micha will always be there—they control me.

"You know, you scared the shit out of me that night," he says, staring at the bathtub. "The way you looked when I found you… I don't ever want to see that look in your eyes again—that emptiness."

222

"It was *my* fault." I let it fall off my chest and crash into the world. "I was supposed to watch her that night, but I was selfish and thought that stupid party was more important."

He turns my head toward him and looks me in the eyes, so I can see how much he means what he says. "You're not selfish. You were seventeen and you made a mistake just like every other seventeen-year-old out there does."

"She died because of my mistake." The words scratch at my throat. "If I would have just stayed home like I was supposed to then she wouldn't be dead."

"You have to let this go," he says, his voice strained. "You can't keep blaming yourself for something that was out of your hands."

"I wish I could have a redo." Tears sting the corners of my eyes. "I want to do it over again."

He covers my hand with his. "I think you might need to talk to someone about this. Otherwise it's going to haunt you forever."

I suck the tears back and wiggle my hand away from his. "You think I'm going crazy."

He shifts in front of me onto his knees, takes my face in his hands, and forces me to look at him. "Look at me. No one thinks you're crazy. You're strong, but you've been through a lot of shit and you might need some help working through it."

"I think I'm more fucked up than you realize," I say. "I can't even look in a mirror anymore."

"That does sound crazy." He tucks my hair out of my face and takes a good look at me. "You're beautiful."

I shake my head slowly. "It's not that. It's something else. Like if I look in the mirror I have to see what's really inside."

"What's inside isn't bad."

"Yes, it is. If you knew the truth, you wouldn't want to be with me."

He assesses me closely and then helps me to my feet, pulling me up by the arms.

"What are you doing?" I ask as he steers me by the shoulders to the mirror on the medicine cabinet. I wince at the girl staring back at me; big green eyes, wet hair stuck to her head, and mascara running down her face. I begin to recoil, but he holds me in place and forces me to look at myself.

His aqua eyes lock on my reflection. "When I saw you that night, I felt completely helpless. I loved being able to help you, whether it's if you fell off the roof and needed to go to the hospital or you needed help climbing up a tree. It has always been my thing since we were kids and I loved every second of it, but that night there was absolutely nothing I could do to help you. I never want to feel that way again." He takes a deep breath and lets it out gradually. "I love you, Ella May and nothing will ever change that. You can push me away—run away—and I will still love you."

Hot tears pour out of my eyes and down my cheeks. My shoulders start to shake as I turn to him and bury my face into his chest. His arms circle around my waist and he lifts me up. My arms and legs fasten around him like he is my lifeline, and maybe he is.

He carries me into my room as I continue to sob and he lies down with me on the bed. It's dark and the music from next door drifts through the open window. Tears spill continuously to downpour from my eyes, and I place my hand over his chest, feeling the beat of his heart. I keep crying years of tears that have been bottled up until finally my eyes run dry.

Then I breathe again.

Micha

I wake up early in morning in a state of panic. Ella is fast asleep in my arms, her eyes swollen from crying, and she's clinging onto me like I'm everything to her. It's what I've always wanted, but something feels unresolved within me and I need to fix it before I get in too deep with her. She needs someone strong and until I face the thing plaguing me, I can't be that for her.

But I will be.

Carefully, I raise her head from my shoulder and slip out of her room. Her dad's snoring on the couch, there's a broken bottle on the kitchen floor, and the back door is wide open. I lock up and then jump the fence. My yard is trashed with beer bottles and cigarette butts and my mom's car is parked in the driveway.

The inside looks just as bad and I feel like a dick for leaving it for my mom to clean up, but if I don't go right now, I'll chicken out. So I hurry to my room, where Ethan's passed out in my bed with his arms and legs hanging over the side. He still has on the clothes from last night and the whole room stinks of stale booze and cigarettes.

I stuff some clothes into a bag and collect my keys from the dresser.

"Are you going somewhere?" Ethan sits up from the bed, rubbing his eyes.

I swing the bag over my shoulder. "I'm going on a little road trip. I'll be back in a few days."

He gapes at me. "By yourself?"

"Yeah, this is something I have to do by myself."

He considers something. "You're going to see your father, aren't you?"

I let out a loud breath. "Yeah man, but don't say anything, okay?"

Ethan nods. "Alright, if that's what you want me to do."

"It is." I open the door. "And hey, help my mom clean up… and keep an eye on Ella."

He falls back into the bed. "Alright man, will do."

I grab my wallet and leave the room, wondering who I'm going to be when I come back.

Ella

I wake up to an empty bed, but try to stay calm. I text Micha and ask him where he is because I'm sure there's an explanation.

"I'm sure it's nothing bad," I say, but there's an unsettling feeling squeezing inside me.

I slip on a pair of shorts and a tank top and go downstairs to head to his house, but Dean, Lila, and a girl with short black hair are sitting at the kitchen table with coffee mugs in front of them. There's a box of doughnuts on the counter and someone's taken out the garbage and cleaned the dishes.

"Oh my God, it's so nice to finally meet you." The girl with black hair stands up and meets me in the middle of the kitchen.

"Likewise, I guess…" I shake her extended hand, glancing at Lila and then Dean.

Dean gets up and brushes crumbs off the front of his button down shirt. "Ella, this is my fiancé, Caroline."

My mouth forms an "O." She's not how I pictured her; short and slender, with tan skin and shoulder length wavy hair. She has a vest on over a t-shirt and a pair of black jeans. There's a butterfly tattoo on her wrist and her ears have multiple piercings. I pictured her more prim and proper, by the way my brother showed up looking.

"Dean's told me so much about you," she says with a genuine smile. "And I'm finally glad to have a face to attach to the stories he's been telling me."

My eyes wander to Dean and my eyebrows arch up. "Stories, huh? I'd love to hear these stories."

She doesn't miss a beat. "Like how you like to draw and how you love cars. He also said you attend UNLV, which is so cool because that's where I went."

"I thought you said you didn't know where I was," I say to Dean.

He shifts uneasily. "Dad told me once during like a five minute conversation. But anyway, it's not a big deal, Ella, for me to tell my fiancé about my little sister."

"It kind of is." My voice carries an underlying meaning that only he will understand. "All things considering."

Dean hisses through clenched teeth. "Ella, can you not start this shit. It's too early in the morning."

Caroline glances from Dean to me then back to Dean. "You weren't lying. You guys' relationship is a little intense."

Removing myself from the conversation, I pull my hair into a ponytail and pour myself a cup of coffee. Breathing in the aroma, I stare out the window, noting that Micha's car isn't next door.

"Where the hell is he?" I mutter to myself.

Suddenly, I'm being yanked by the arm out of the room.

"Hey," I protest as hot coffee spills onto my foot. "What is your problem?"

"Look." Dean says once we're in the living room. "I didn't invite her here. She just showed up to surprise me."

"So you don't want her here?" I take a sip of my coffee, hiding my amusement.

He rubs the back of his neck tensely. "There's just stuff she doesn't know about me yet and I don't think I'm ready to tell her."

"You told her about me."

"But not dad. And not mom either."

229

I set the cup down on the table and wipe up the coffee from my foot with a towel. "Okay, so what do you want to do about it?"

"Could you hang out with her for the day, while I pack up the rest of my room?" he asks. "And then I can get her out of here by tomorrow morning."

"You should just tell her the truth." I toss the towel on the couch. "Avoiding the problem will only catch up with you."

He pulls an annoyed face. "You're one to talk."

"I know and I'm working on it." My voice shakes a little and I clear it.

His face is turning red. "Would you please just keep her busy?"

"I guess." I shrug. "But where do you want me to take her?"

"For a drive around the lake or something," he says. "I don't care just as long as you keep her away from here."

I collect my coffee and proceed for the kitchen, while he heads for the stairs to finish packing.

"And Ella," he calls out from the stairway "You look different today—happier."

I give him a small smile, and then I turn away, wondering what looks different.

Chapter 17

Micha

I called my dad from the road and got his address. He tried to talk to me a little bit, but I hung up on him. Confronting him for bailing is not something I'm going to do over the phone.

He lives about two hours away, which pisses me off. Two hours away and he hasn't stopped by once. When I pull up to his house, my hands nearly choke the life out of the steering wheel. He lives in a two-story white-brick mansion. The neighborhood is nice with gigantic houses and people walking their dogs along the sidewalk. There's no drug dealings going on, no fights, no junky cars parked in the front yard.

I sit in my car staring at the red door with a big "Welcome" sign hanging on it. There are flowers around the front of the yard and the grass is green and cut. Is this why he left us? Because he wanted a fancier life. Why the fuck couldn't he do that with us?

My phone beeps in my pocket and I turn it off. It's Ella and I can't talk to her right now.

The front door opens and a man in his forties steps out onto the porch. His hair is the same color of blonde as mine, but thinner. He's wearing a black suit and looks like an arrogant prick.

He scoops up the newspaper from the ground and squints at my car as he trots off the porch. I count to five in my head, force my hands away from the steering wheel, and get out of the car. He recognizes me immediately and his face drains of color.

"Micha?" He tucks the newspaper under his arm. "Is that you?"

I take another deep breath and walk across the front lawn. "I don't even know why I'm here."

"Why don't you come inside so we can talk?" he suggests. I follow him into the house that's even nicer on the inside; hardwood floors, a massive chandelier, and freshly painted walls with family pictures on them. "You have a family?"

He tosses the newspaper onto a table and motions for me to have a seat in the living room. "Yeah, a daughter that's twelve and a son that's eight."

Feeling awkward, I sit down in a chair that's decorated with frilly pillows. He seats himself across from me, seeming like he has no idea what to do or say next. "So how have you been?"

"Super." There's a large portrait on the wall taken in a church of him and his wife on their wedding day and I stare at it, doing the math. "How long have you been remarried?"

He fidgets uncomfortably as he leans back in the chair and stations his foot onto his knee. "Micha, look I'd rather not get into this."

"What did you do? Like run out on us and marry the first person you came across?" Anger burns in my voice. He looks away toward the window and I get it. "You were seeing her while you were still with mom, weren't you?"

He makes eye contact with me again, with eyes exactly like mine. "Look Micha, there were things going on between your mother and I that you don't understand... I wasn't happy."

"There were things going on between you and me, too," I snap. "So what's your excuse for that one?"

He rubs a hand across his face and lets out an exhausted sigh. "I'm sorry."

I clench my hands into fists, fighting the urge to jump off the couch and strangle him. "You're *sorry*? Great answer, asshole."

He snatches a manila folder out of the drawer of the end table and slams it down on the coffee table between us. "Your grandfather left you some money in his will."

My eyes flash from the folder to my father. "Is that why you brought me here?"

He opens the folder and takes a small stack of papers out. "I thought maybe you could use it to go to college or something. That would be nice, wouldn't it?"

Shaking my head, I get to my feet. "I'm not going to college and you'd understand that if you knew me past the age of six."

He slides the papers across the table and sets a pen next to them. "Please just take the money, Micha. I want to know that you're taken care of otherwise it'll haunt me."

I pause. "Are you planning on ever seeing me again?" His silence gives me the only answer I need. "I don't want your God damn money." I throw the papers at him and storm for the front door. "Give it to one of your real kids."

He doesn't call after me when I stomp out the door and he doesn't chase me down. I march straight for my car, getting more furious with each step, and I slam my fist into the driver's side window. It doesn't break, but a couple of my knuckles pop.

"Fuck!" I shout, clutching my hand and the old lady across the street, who's working in her garden, scurries inside her mansion.

I jump in my car and speed off down the road with no idea where the hell I'm going.

Chapter 18

Ella

Micha won't text me back and it's eating away at my mind. I need to find out where he is, but Caroline's making it difficult. She's a photographer and wants to take pictures of the different views of our town. I take her to the lake first because it's the sunnier side of town, and pull over in a few different turnouts that give her various views. When we reach the bridge, she gets really enthusiastic and wants pictures of it too.

"It has so much history to it," she says. "And it probably carries a lot of memories for people."

I wonder if Caroline is a mind reader on top of a photographer.

A thin cloud of dust surrounds us as I tap the brakes and park the car just at the brink of the bridge and she hops out with her camera bag on her shoulder. Lila and I trek after her, taking our sweet time, but I halt at the line that splits the road from the bridge.

"So is this *the* bridge?" Lila asks, watching me through her sunglasses.

I stare at the spot on the ground where Micha and I stood kissing in the rain. "Yeah, this is the bridge." With a quiver in my heart, I step onto the concrete and walk up to the railing. Gripping the bar, I gaze out at the lake, glistening in the sunlight, so much brighter than that rainy night.

Caroline clicks her camera, getting the lake at every angle while Lila roams to the other side. The wind blows through my hair and I shut my eyes, going back to that night. I'd been cleaning out my mom's medicine cabinet earlier that morning and had come across the bottle of pills she'd taken to keep her delusions under control. I'd wondered if they'd worked for her and how they made her mind see life. So I took one to see for myself and then headed off with Micha to a party.

As soon as I'd climbed in his car, he'd sensed something was off with me. "You look out of it," he said. "Maybe we should just stay in tonight."

I shook my head and motioned for him to drive. Frowning, he drove us to the party, but he kept a close eye on me almost the entire night, following me like a puppy. Usually, I didn't mind, but I grew restless with the desire to figure out what the hell my mother was thinking. So when Micha got preoccupied by a girl, I cornered Grantford and asked him to drive me to the bridge. He had happily obliged, thinking he was going to get some.

When we arrived at the bridge it was raining buckets of water. I thanked him politely and told him he could go. He was pissed and started yammering something about why the hell did he drive me out here.

I shrugged and slammed the door shut, stepping out into the rain. He spun away from the bridge, the tires of his pickup kicking up gravel and mud all over my boots. I walked over to the railing and stepped up onto the curb, observing the water through the veil of rain. But it wasn't close enough, so I stepped up onto the beam just like I remembered her doing.

It still didn't make sense why she did it—why she thought she could fly and I don't think it ever will.

I jerk away from my reminiscing and concentrate on Caroline, who's still snapping pictures, with the long lens of her camera close to my face.

"You're a deep thinker," she remarks and clicks her camera again. "And you photograph well."

I shake my head. "No, I'm not. Not really."

She snaps another picture and moves the camera away. "As a photographer I get to see through a totally different eye. I think it makes me see people differently— more clearly."

"Like a mirror?"

"Yeah, kind of."

She turns the lens toward the lake and starts snapping pictures of it. I recline against the railing and scroll through my messages. I only have one, Micha's voicemail from a few weeks ago. I decide maybe it's time.

I press dial and put it up to my ear.

"Hey Ella, it's Micha," he says nervously, unlike himself, and sighs "Well, that was a stupid opening line, so pretend you didn't hear that."

A smile tugs at the corners of my lips. That sounds more like him.

"Anyway, I'm kind of irritated that you just took off and haven't called." He pauses and I can hear Ethan in the background. "Actually, I'm fucking pissed off. I don't even know what to say. You just bail after everything we've been through. Do you know how crazy I've been wondering where you were or if you were even alive?

My heart compresses in my chest. I've never heard him so upset.

"You just bailed out on everyone and people need you, even if you don't think so. Grady's sick—he has cancer and..." He inhales a shaky breath. "I still love you... I don't know what else to say and there's probably not even a point of saying anymore... you won't call me back."

It clicks and the message ends. It's not what I was imagining. I'd never once looked at it from his side—how worried he must have been. I send him another text, but again, he doesn't respond.

***

One week passes and I still don't hear from Micha. He won't call me or answer my texts, and his phone is going straight to voicemail. His mom has no idea where he is either and she's starting to get really worried.

Ever since I returned from the bridge, little images of what happened when Micha picked me up that night have been flickering through my head. Something infinite happened that night, not with Micha, but with me.

I arrive at the conclusion, while I'm sitting out on my porch, staring at his vacant driveway, that it's time to get to the bottom of what's going on with Micha. There is only one person I could think of who might know where he is. Ethan. And I need backup.

"What are we trying to get out of him?" Lila asks as I drive up to the shop Ethan works at.

"Where Micha is." I tell her, putting the shifter into park. "And I think Ethan might know."

Her forehead scrunches as she eyes the open garage door. Ethan is behind a car being worked on, tossing a screwdriver and catching it like a baseball. "But why am I here?"

"Because you're my backup."

"And what exactly is it you want me to do?"

"I'm not sure yet." I bite my nail, assessing the situation.

Ethan is dressed in a nice pair of jeans and plaid button-down shirt, not his work clothes, which means he can leave if he wants to and he probably will, making this as difficult as possible. Especially if Micha told him not to tell me.

He tips his head back and laughs at something his dad said. Then his eyes find my dad's Firebird and his expression drops. I open the door and he throws down the tool and runs through the shop. I jog across the gravel and swing open the front door, leaving Lila behind.

Sitting behind the counter is Mrs. Gregory, Ethan's mother who has the same dark hair and brown eyes as Ethan. She looks up quickly from a magazine and her eyes brighten.

"Ella, is that you?" She gets up from the stool and rounds the counter to give me a hug. "I didn't know you were back, honey."

"For the summer, I am." My eyes skim the room and the shop. "Is Ethan in there?"

She points over her shoulder. "He just ran back into the storage room. You want me to go get him?"

"Would you mind if I did?" I ask politely.

"Sure, hun." She steps aside and lets me behind the counter.

The storage room is lined with rows and rows of shelves holding parts for cars. It's quiet, dark, and the sink has a drip.

"Ethan," I say, shutting the door quietly behind me. "I know you're in here."

"I hear a shuffle from the back corner diagonal from me. I hurry down the tire aisle, peeking through the shelf, and catch him running up the other side. I skitter backwards, hoping to cut him off at the end by the door.

"Ethan will you please talk to me?" My voice echoes back at me. Looking left then right, I exit the aisle. "Look, I know he told you where he went, so will you please just tell me… or at least tell me if he's okay."

He suddenly reveals himself from an aisle a few rows down. "He told me not to tell you where he was."

I press my lips together at the sting in my heart. "I need to know. I'm worried about him."

He props his elbow on the edge of a shelf. "Well, now you know how he's felt for the last eight months."

The painful feeling of reality sinks in. "Please, please, will you just tell me where he is. It's killing me not knowing."

He eyes me over, like he's hunting for my sincerity. "He went to see his dad."

My jaw almost hits the floor. "When did he find out where his dad was?"

Ethan sighs and leans against the shelf. "He started calling the house a few weeks ago, asking to talk to Micha. Micha wouldn't talk to him, but then a few days ago, he finally decided it was time to go see him."

"Is he still with his dad?" I ask.

He hesitates. "No... Let's just say the visit didn't go very well."

I force the lump in my throat down. "Is he okay?"

"I'm not sure....He was staying with some of our old friends over at Farrows Park the last time I talked to him."

"Is he coming back?"

"Again, I'm not sure."

I sink to the cold concrete floor and let my head fall into my hands. "Why didn't he tell me?"

Ethan puffs out a loud breath and sits down beside me. "Because he didn't want you dealing with his problems on top of your own. He worries about you all the time. It's kind of annoying." I raise my head and scowl at him. He chuckles and nudges me with his elbow. "What? I'm the one who's had to listen to him talk about you for the last eight months. At one point, I almost stabbed my ears out just so I didn't have to hear it."

I give a gentle pat to his knee. "Pretend all you want. You're not as bad of a guy as you want people to think."

He comprehends the deeper meaning to my words. "Yeah, yeah, say what you want, but deep down, I'm just your average douche bag, like every other guy out there."

Laughing, we get up and go out to the lobby, where there's a guy waiting at the front counter. He walks me to the door and stares out at Lila sitting out on the hood of my car examining her watch.

"So what are you going to do?" he asks as I push open the door.

"I'm not sure yet," I say. "I doubt you're going to tell me where the house is that he's staying at."

"I don't think it'd be a good idea for you to go there. He needs to clear his head." He backs up toward the register with his hands stuffed into his pockets. "I got customers to take care of."

I meet Lila at the car and she slides off the hood. "Did he tell you anything?"

We climb in the car and I quickly explain to her the vague details of what happened.

"So where are we going?" she asks, buckling her seatbelt.

The sunlight sparkles through the windshield and into my eyes. "We're going home."

***

A couple more days drag by and I still don't hear anything from Micha. It baffles me how much I miss him, but I do my best to keep busy, not wanting to get sucked up in the loneliness and worry.

Dean and Caroline went home about a week ago. Caroline told me they'd come back to visit before the summer was over or she would at least see me again at the wedding, which is in October.

Lila is out for the day with Ethan, not on a date, something they both insisted when I brought it up. My dad is locked in his room. He had a rough night and got into a fight. I received a call from Denny at two o'clock in the morning telling me to come pick him up. Deciding I need a break from my house, I peek in on my dad who is fast asleep, and then drive over to Grady's house. Amy's car is parked in front of the trailer and the front door is wide open, swaying in the wind a little.

I hop out of the car as she walks outside with a bag over her shoulder and a box of Grady's stuff in her arms.

I fear the worst has happened. "Is everything okay?"

She sighs, transferring the box to the side of her hip to free her hand so she can get the car door open. "He caught a bad case of pneumonia and he's been taken to the hospital over in Monroe."

I brace my hand on the trunk of the car for support. "Is he okay?"

Shaking her head, she sets the box on the seat and slams the door shut with her hip. "His body's already fightin' cancer. This just makes things worse."

"I need to go see him," I mumble and turn for my car.

"He can't have visitors right now, Ella," she says empathetically. "His immune system's too low."

I frown. "Will you let me know when he can?"

She gives me a small smile, but there's something in her eyes I don't like. "Yeah, hun. I will."

As I back down the driveway, watching her lock up, I feel helpless and out-of-control. I want to run away, back to Vegas, or somewhere else equally as far away, so I won't have to feel it.

But I don't.

***

I try not to stress too much about Grady, but my thoughts keep drifting to him. Whether he's in a hospital bed with sterilized walls? Or did Amy take a box of his stuff to fix it up for him?

"What song is this?" Lila is lying on her stomach in my bed, flipping through the pages of a magazine.

"'Black Sun' by *Jo Mango*," I say, sharpening one of my charcoal pencils over the garbage in my bedroom.

"It's sad." She frowns, resting her chin in her hand. "It makes me want to cry."

"It's a good song to draw to." I return to my drawing on the floor. The dark lines of it form pieces of a shattered mirror and I start sketching a picture of a guitar inside one of them. When I'm done, each piece will hold something about my life, but it might take me a while to finish it.

Lila raises her head away from her hand and glances at the window. "Did you hear that?"

There's shouting coming from outside, loud enough to be heard over the music.

I shade one of the corners with my pinky. "It's probably just the neighbors."

The yelling gets louder and Lila sits up nervously and draws back the curtain. "Ella, there's a man and a woman fighting out in front of the driveway."

I set my pencil down on the floor and go over to the window. There's a short, fat man and a tall, slender woman yelling at each other just outside the boundaries of my front yard.

"That's the Anderson's," I explain. "They always do that."

"We should stop it," she says worriedly. "He might hurt her."

"I'll take care of it," I tell her. "You stay here."

I pad down the stairs, barefoot and in my boxer shorts and tank top, and poke my head out the door, but the Anderson's have vanished from the street.

The lyrics and music of "Behind Blue Eyes" by *The Who* is blasting from the stereo in Micha's room next door. It's his sad mood song, the one he lets play over and over again when he's depressed.

The lights aren't on in the house, but the one in the garage shines brightly into the night. Sticking out of the open door is the back end of his Chevelle. There's a large dent in the bumper that wasn't there when he left and a scratch on the corner of the fender.

Walking down the steps the concrete is ice-cold against my bare feet. I spot him through the window of the garage, searching the shelf for something with a cigarette in his mouth. I watch him move, my pulse instantly speeding up, and I have to work to keep breathing.

As he pulls away from the shelf with a box in his hand, he turns his head toward the window, like he senses me out here. Our eyes lock and collide. He sets the box down and disappears out of my view.

A few seconds later he walks out of the garage. His jeans ride low on his hips and the porch light hits his chest, highlighting his well-defined muscles and the cursive font of the tattoo on his rib.

"When did you start smoking again?" I inquire from my driveway.

He takes the cigarette out of his mouth with his eyes on me. "I slipped up a few days ago... There's just too much going on, I guess."

I take a few small steps across the driveway and my heart thuds in my chest. "Is it because of your dad?"

Micha reaches the grass, just before the fence divides our houses. "How do you know about that?"

I stop just short of the fence and wrap my arms around myself to keep warm. "Ethan told me."

He shakes his head, annoyed. "He's worse than a girl."

"Hey." I feign offense, attempting to lighten his mood. "Not all girls are bad. I've always been an excellent secret keeper. You know that."

He places his hands on the fence and clutches at the links. "I don't know if that's true anymore." He gestures his hand at me. "Maybe this was who you always were. Maybe this place was just getting in the way of you."

He's upset and I need to get to the bottom of why. "You could have told me about your dad."

"Could I of?" The front of his thighs push against the fence. "I don't think you can handle it right now — you can barely handle your own problems."

I reduce the small gap left between the fence and myself. "Try me."

His eyes examine my face, looking for something deep within me. Then his head falls down, defeated, and he lets out a slow breath. "It was almost as painful as that day you ran off. I mean, he has a whole other fucking family…." His voice cracks and he clears his throat. "Like we weren't good enough or something."

The ache in his voice nearly kills me. I close my eyes and tell myself I can do this—that I'm the strong one at the moment. My eyes open and I put my finger under his chin, forcing him to look at me. His eyes are glassy, like he's about to cry, and he tries to look away. I place an unsteady hand on his cheek and maintain his gaze.

"I know it hurts right now," I say, grappling my voice even. "But it will get better. It'll just take some time and I'll be here for you this time. I promise."

He looks unconvinced. Not knowing what else to say, I stand on my tiptoes, lean over the fence, and lightly graze my lips across his. Heat caresses my mouth and skin.

"I need you right now," Micha murmurs against my lips with so much desire in his eyes that my knees buckle. "I need this right now."

His hand cups around the back of my neck, much gentler than the intensity in his voice, and he crashes my body against his. He tempts me with a soft brush of his lips and every ounce of sexual tension between us explodes. I can't help myself—I fall into him.

250

My lips part willingly, lost in the mind-numbing moment as he slips his tongue deep inside my mouth, devouring me thoroughly. He tastes like cigarettes mingled with mint and the scent of his cologne is intoxicating.

My hands trace up the front of his bare chest, and I loop my arms around his neck. The links of the fence dig into my skin as we crush it between our bodies, trying to bury ourselves into one another. Micha pulls away for a second and my lips falter in protest, but he lifts me up over the fence and encourages my legs around his waist. My inner thighs burn as they graze his hips. Every part of him touches me and it makes my body flame. I arch into him, moaning as his lips return to mine even more ravenously.

"Oh my God, this feels so good." He groans, before heading toward his house.

"What are you doing?" I whisper against his lips, knowing where he's going, but I'm not sure I'm ready for it yet.

"Shh…" His warm tongue slips deep inside my mouth and I forget about arguing.

His hands hold me up by the ass as he kicks the back door open and stumbles into his kitchen. He knocks over a lamp and bumps into the wall as he carries me blindly down the hall and into his room. Then we collapse on the bed, tangled together. The music is loud and he reaches over to the stereo and turns it down so it filters through the room softly.

"Ow," I squeal, squirming. "Something just poked me."

"I'm pretty sure that's supposed to happen," Micha jokes with feral eyes.

I swat his chest and reach underneath me, retrieving a drumstick. He snatches it from my hand, laughing softly as he chucks it over his shoulder and it lands somewhere in the dark.

His face turns serious as he smoothes my hair back, looking into my eyes so passionately, my nerves crack through. "Do you know I realized I loved you when we were like sixteen? But I didn't want to tell you because I was afraid you'd run away."

I prop up on my elbows, making our faces inches away. Strands of his hair hang in my face. "But I was normal back then. Or at least partly normal."

He lets his forehead rest against mine. "Yeah, but I thought that's how things were supposed to happen when people were in love."

I realize how bad I must have hurt him when I ran off after he tried to tell me he loved me. "Micha, I'm sorry."

His jaw spasms and he tips his head back up. When he kisses me again, it feels different somehow—more intimate. My apprehension starts to emerge, but I choke it down and let my head fall back against the pillow. His lips follow mine and he kisses all the fear out of me. My chest presses into his as my neck arches against his trail of kisses along my skin, sucking and nipping at it all the way down.

"Fuck," he groans when his mouth reaches the curve of my breast. The fabric of my tank top is thin and I don't have a bra on. Hesitantly, his tongue lightly slides between my breasts. Instantly, my nipples harden and an irrepressible moan escapes from my lips as desire takes over my body.

I sit up, stunning him, and he moves back.

"What's wrong?" he asks.

Sucking in a deep breath of air, I shut my eyes and wiggle my shirt off. My chest heaves, bare and exposed, as my lungs strain for air. I've never been this far with a guy before—never wanted to. Getting close to someone meant getting attached and getting attached has only brought me hurt in the past. But Micha's different. He always has been. I just didn't realize it until now.

He takes me in deliberately and then covers his body with mine, colliding our bare chest together as we collapse back onto the mattress. My fingers tangle in his soft hair as his hands travel down my shoulders to my breasts. My back bows up, seeking to feed a starvation inside my body, but unsure how to do it. Pausing, I curve my hips and rub up against him. A shot of ecstasy swells through my body and a gasp fumbles from my lips.

Hearing the unrestrained noise sends me into a state of anxiety and I fall back to reality. I'm not sure if my mind is ready to go where my body obviously wants to—whether I can allow myself to completely let go.

"Micha wait," I say in a strained voice.

He jerks back quickly, his hand still cupping my breast. "What is it?"

"I'm sorry. I just can't... I don't think I'm ready yet."

He kisses my forehead tenderly and boosts up on his elbows, his body still hovering over me. With his fingertip, he sketches a line from my temple to my jaw and my eyelids flutter. "Will you let me try one more thing?"

I open my eyes, dazed from his touch. "I'm not sure if I can go any farther tonight."

"Just trust me, okay?" he says. "And if it gets to be too much, just say and I promise I'll stop."

I bite at my lip, knowing where he's going with this. "Okay."

Unhurriedly, with his eyes fastened on mine, he moves his mouth and kisses the hollow of my neck, sending shivers over my skin. His lips move downward and linger just above my breast. My eyes shut as his mouth touches my nipple and his tongue slips out over it. He sucks on it hard and I swear to God I can't breathe. My legs vice-grip around him and the longer he devours me, the fiercer his mouth gets. With each movement of his tongue, my thighs burn hotter.

I need... something. "Micha, I..."

"Shh..." he whispers and trails rapturous kisses up my neck. "I'll take care of it."

His fingers slide down my bare stomach and to the bottom of my shorts, leaving a path of heat along my skin. As his lips find mine again, his finger slips deep inside me. The lyrics of the music fade away as my panic bursts into a thousand blissful pieces.

Micha

When Ella screams out my name, with her head tipped back, her eyes lost, it's unlike anything I've ever experienced before. She trusted me enough to do things to her that no one else has and it makes me feel alive again.

Of course, my dick is so hard it actually hurts.

"Behind Blue Eyes" by *The Who* is stuck on repeat and fills up the moment. It's the song I turn on when I feel down, but I don't think it's going to be that anymore—not after tonight.

I brush her hair away from her forehead. "Are you okay?"

Her green eyes are glazed over as she nods her head up and down. There's a look on her face that brings a smile to my lips. "I'm better than fine." She leans up and kisses me.

I draw her in, intensifying the kiss, then let her go, needing to cool down. "You should stay here tonight."

I expect her to protest, but she nods as she tugs her shirt back over her head. "Okay, but I'll have to use your phone to text Lila. I didn't bring mine with me."

I kiss her forehead, then her temple, breathing her in. "I'm gonna go take a shower. I'll be right back."

Confining a laugh, she reaches for my phone on my nightstand. "A cold one?"

I grab some clothes out of my dresser and back out the doorway. "You better watch it, Ella May. Or I may decide against it and you'll just have to deal with me for the rest of the night."

She flops back on the bed as she sends a text. "Maybe that's what I'm hoping for."

Shaking my head, I throw my clothes on the floor and jump onto the bed, putting a knee on each side of her. She laughs as I playfully trap her arms above her head. I move my lips next to her ear and gently take a nip at her. I breathe on her neck, letting my warm breath cause her to shudder, teasing her and driving both our bodies crazy.

She lets out a moan and I feel her legs start to move around me.

Sighing, I pull away before I get even more wound up. "Okay, I have to go take a shower." I climb off the bed, watching her all the way to the door.

Once I'm out of the room, all of the pain I've been feeling about my dad smothers me again, but all I can do is keep breathing.

Chapter 19

Ella

The next day is lighter somehow, like I've been buried in the sand and someone has finally dug me out. Micha seems happier too, although I can tell he's still hurting, so I work on keeping his mind distracted.

"So what did you do to it?" I ask Micha as I circle the back end of his car with my hands on my hips, taking in the scratches and dings in the black paint, which look worse in the sunlight.

"I took it for a very intense joy ride." A lazy grin stretches across his face as he puts his head beneath the hood to examine the engine.

I plant my butt on the edge where he's working and cross my leg over my knee. "At least tell me you won? And that the scratches and dings were totally worth it."

"Of course. They're always worth it," he says with a hidden meaning that only the two of us could ever understand.

Gripping the edge, I lean back over the engine and give him a peck on the cheek. He grins, tosses a greasy rag onto the ground, and pinches my ass. A squeak comes out of my mouth as I jump from the pinch and fall toward the engine. Pushing myself back up, I get grease all over my arms and backside. I hop off the hood, trying to clean the grease off with my hands, but it's only making a bigger mess.

Micha laughs at me as he retrieves a new tool box from the top shelf. "That's a good look for you."

I stick out my tongue and turn to leave.

"Where are you going?" he asks.

I hold up my greasy hands. "Thanks to you, I have to go take a shower and wash my clothes."

A wicked look dances in his eyes. "I have grease all over me to. I think I may need to come in there with you."

My stomach flips thinking about last night. I keep backing up toward my house with my eyes on him. "I'll tell you what. If you can catch me, you can shower with me."

His eyes scroll my body as he sucks his lip ring in between his teeth. "Is that a challenge, pretty girl?"

I try not to smile as I exit the garage into the sunlight, but it's too much and my lips turn upward. I take off toward my house and his footsteps head after me. I jump the fence gracefully, but by the time I reach the back door, his arms are circling my waist. He spins me around and picks me up effortlessly. Hooking my legs around his waist, he opens the door and gets us into the kitchen.

He glances around the room and cocks an eyebrow. "Is Lila here?"

I shake my head slowly. "She's with Ethan."

"What about your dad?"

"He went to work."

His aqua eyes darken and I can't help but kiss him. I feel him walking, traveling somewhere as our tongues entwine together. I run my fingers through his hair grabbing onto as much of him as possible, shutting my fear away and basking in the moment.

Without breaking his lips away from mine, he carries me into the downstairs bathroom. When I hear the shower water turn on, I pull my lips away from his. Before I can ask what he's doing, he sets me down underneath the warm water.

I let out a scream as my clothes are drenched.

"See, this way you're washing your clothes and taking a shower at the same time." He grins and tips the shower-head down so it hits more of me.

I seize the front of his T-shirt and yank him forward, so he stumbles into the running water. He braces his hands on the walls, and water sprays over his hair and drips down his face.

I smile at him innocently and allow the water to stream down my body. "Now you're all clean too."

He shakes his head, then shoves away from the wall and jumps all the way into the shower with me. He shuts the curtain and seals us inside the steam. His jeans and T-shirt are sopping wet and beads of water drip into his eyes. I run my hand across his forehead over a spot of grease and then through his hair. He aims the shower head down on me and I tip my head back into the flow. He combs his fingers through my hair sensually and his other hand comes down on the wall behind me as he gathers some of my hair into his hand. Pulling at the roots, he leads me toward him for a deep, watery kiss. Steam surrounds us and makes the passion inside my body ignite.

Panic starts screaming inside my head, but I tell it to shut up and suck the water off his lips as I find the bottom of his shirt to lift it over his head. He pulls back and helps me out, slipping it off and tossing it to the side, instantly reuniting his lips with mine. My fingers trace along the lines of his muscles and the pattern of the tattoo on his rib cage; the lyrics to the first song he ever wrote.

His hands explore my hips, my waist, then up my shirt. Finally, I just take it off for him and then he unhooks my bra. Our bare chests crash together as we continue to kiss underneath the hot water. Minutes later, the rest of our clothes are in a pile by our feet and I can hardly think straight. The way he touches me, kisses me—nothing has ever felt like this before.

He sucks on my breast and licks the water off my skin on my bare stomach, continuing to go down until his tongue finds the right spot. I fall back against the wall as a scream claws up my throat and I lose total control over my body.

This time I don't mind.

Micha

After Ella comes apart, I turn the water off and grab a towel off the hook. She raises her arms above her head, keeping her eyes on me as I wrap the towel around her.

"What?" I ask her, because I can tell she's thinking deeply about something.

"Nothing." She shrugs casually, but her cheeks turn a little pink. "It's just that if I would have known all along that it felt that good, I probably wouldn't have fought it so hard."

"Well, I'm glad you think I'm that good," I tease her snatching another towel and tying it around my waist.

She nibbles on her lip apprehensively as she crosses her arms and rests back against the wall.

"Alright, pretty girl," I demand. "What are you thinking about?"

She lets her lip pop free. "It just doesn't seem fair that I'm the one that gets to have all the fun."

I try not to get too excited, because let's face it, she's a runner. "I'm sure I'll have plenty of fun by myself later."

She reaches forward hesitantly and yanks the towel off my waist.

"That was smooth," I say, gripping the edge of the counter, fighting to stay calm.

Her eyes travel over my body. "I learned from the best." She runs her fingers softly along my swollen cock, making me harder than I already am.

"Fuck, Ella," I say, leaning back against the door and letting go.

Ella

I have no idea what the hell came over me and I'm not going to over analyze it. I can finally breathe again and that's all that matters. Letting things take their course might be exactly what we both need.

Micha wraps a towel around his waist looking happier than I've ever seen him. He kisses me, sucking my bottom lip gently into his mouth, before pulling away and staring into my eyes. "You're so beautiful."

Smiling, I stare down at our wet clothes balled up in the corner. "Now what do we do?"

He licks his lips and braces his hands on the wall, trapping my head between his arms. "We could do it again."

I swat his chest, pretending that he's being silly, even though I do want to do it again. "I mean how do we get out of here? Our clothes are soaking wet and I'm not putting mine back on."

He shrugs and leans away. "No one's home so keep the towel on you and run upstairs."

I eye over his lean chest. "Yeah, but what about you?"

"You can go get me some clothes after you get dressed... if you want to." His lips tug into a flirty grin.

I start to say something, but the back door slams shut and Lila and Ethan's voices float from the kitchen.

"Well, there goes that plan," Micha says with laughter in his tone.

I tighten the towel around me and we wait for them to leave, but after a while, it's clear they're not going anywhere.

"I'll go out there," Micha says and heads for the door.

I pull him back by the arm. "You're in a towel."

"Obviously."

"But they'll see you and know something was up."

He cocks his head to the side, his eyes scrutinizing me. "Is that a bad thing?"

I hug my arms around myself. "No, it's just that... what are we going to tell them we were doing?"

"I'm sure they'll figure it out," he says. "Why is this upsetting you?"

"It's not," I reply, deciding to just be honest. "It's just that... this is like the realest thing I've had in a long time and it scares me a bit."

He tucks a strand of my damp hair out of my eyes. "I know it does, but you'll be okay—*we'll* be okay."

I nod quickly and then move away from the wall, straightening my shoulders. "Are you coming back after you change?"

He plants a kiss on my forehead. "Where else would I go?"

I move out of his way and he walks out the door in his towel, like he's not embarrassed at all. He leaves the door cracked behind him and seconds later I hear the sound of Lila's shocked voice followed by the laughter of Ethan. A few seconds later footsteps head my way.

"Oh Ella," Lila says through the crack in the door. "Can I come in?"

Holding the towel on, I open the door about half way. "Could you go get me some clothes, please? Mine are soaking wet."

She covers her mouth, stifling her laughter. "Sure. I'll be right back."

She comes back with a pair of red shorts and a grey tank top. I get dressed and we meet Micha and Ethan out in the garage. Micha's wearing a pair of loose fitted jeans and his favorite Pink Floyd t-shirt, and he tries not to smirk when he sees me, but Ethan doesn't hold back.

"Have fun this morning?" he asks me and I punch him in the arm.

"Ow," he fakes hurt and then glances down at the engine. "Dude, you ripped this thing to shit. What the fuck did you do to it?"

"I took it down to Taylor Bay and drag raced it," he says with a shrug. "I guess I pushed it too hard."

"Then where'd the dents come from?" I question, peering underneath the hood.

"I had an unfortunate run in with another car," he says, with a twinkle in his eye as he captures my gaze. "But I still won."

Ethan sighs and slams the hood shut. "Get in and we'll take it to the shop."

We pile into the car and Micha drives it up on the grass to maneuver it around Ethan's truck parked in the

266

center of the driveway. We drive down the road toward the shop holding hands over the console, listening to Lila and Ethan chat about their day, something so simple, but so meaningful.

When Micha pauses at a stop sign, Mikey's cherry red Camaro rolls up to the side of us. He points at Micha's car and then one of his friends mockingly waves.

"Fucking asshole," Ethan mutters from the backseat.

I roll down the window. "Is there a problem?"

Mikey laughs and aims a finger at the hood. "What'd ya do to that poor thing? It sounds like it's dying."

"It sounds a lot better than your piece of shit car on a good day," I retort, sitting up and sticking my head out the window.

"Ella," Lila says from the backseat, shocked.

"Let her go," Ethan says. "She's very entertaining when she gets this way."

Mikey's greasy black hair shines in the sun as he pokes his head out of the car. "You can keep talking, but it ain't going to do no good since you're both too chicken shit to race me. You guys proved that at the last race."

"Only because your small size was unimpressive," I say with an innocent bat of my eyelashes.

That pisses him off. He jumps out of the car and Micha pulls me back in and leans over the console, resting an arm around my shoulder protectively, knowing that

Mikey's the kind of guy that would hit a girl. Mikey glances up the street before crouching down next to the door.

"If you two think you're so tough then prove it," he says with a venomous tone. "The Back Road, nine o'clock."

"I'm pretty sure she already explained to you that your car isn't worth our time," Micha says evenly. "So back the fuck off and get back in your car."

"The Back Road, nine o'clock," he repeats slowly before backing away and climbing into his car. "And I'm sure with the noises your car's making, it should be a pretty fair race."

He revs his engine, proving something, before speeding off through the intersection, leaving tire marks on the asphalt.

"What a jerk," Lila says from the backseat. "Getting in your face like that—who does that?"

I turn to Micha with a guilty face. "I'm sorry."

He delicately sketches his finger along my lips and sighs. "It's okay. We'll figure something out... Besides you can make it up to me later."

"We can't fix your car that fast, man." Ethan leans over the console, shoving the sleeves of his black shirt up to his elbows, revealing several tattoos on his arms. "It's nowhere close to being in racing condition."

"I know," Micha replies and starts driving again. "I guess we'll just have to go in there blind."

"It could fall apart if you push it too hard," Ethan cautions. "Then you'd be back to square one with it."

"Wait a minute." Lila holds up her hands in front of her. "You guys aren't seriously going to race him, are you?"

"We have to," Ethan and Micha say at the same time.

Lila glances at me for an explanation. "Why?"

Ethan slumps back in the seat and brings his knee up as he turns to Lila. "It's how things work around here. If we don't, then we'll get hounded for it for the rest of our lives."

"Okay..." Lila says jolting in the seat as the car hits a pothole. "What's wrong with that?"

Ethan rifles for a way to explain it to her, brushing his dark hair out of his eyes. "It'd be like getting picked on every day in school by everyone in the school."

Lila tucks her hands under her legs. "That doesn't sound very fun."

"Exactly, so you can understand why we have to race." He folds his arms and directs his attention back to Micha. "Go to the shop, man and we'll see what we can get fixed before it's time to go."

Chapter 20

Ella

"So is this what you used to do all the time?" Lila relaxes back in the lawn chair. "Just sit around and watch them work on cars all day? God, that must have been nice."

I slurp on my Icee, my eyes fastened on Micha and Ethan working on the car on the opposite side of the garage. They're trying to work too fast and it's making me nervous. "No, I used to work on the cars with them."

She dumps a bag of M&M's into her hand. "Do you want to go help them right now?"

"I can hang out here with you," I say and stick out my hand. "Besides, I'm kind of enjoying myself."

She dumps some candy into my hand and I pour the chocolate into my mouth.

"I know you are." She sets the candy on the floor and picks up her soda. "You're practically glowing."

I rest my face in my hand to hide the alleged glowing. "This makes me nervous."

"What does?"

"Racing when the car's not running good."

Lila pulls her hair out of the ponytail and tousles it with her fingers. "Why? Can something go wrong?"

"With racing, anything can go wrong," I say, mad at myself for getting Micha into this mess.

Micha

I kick a tool box out of the way and step up onto the bumper, staring down at the engine. "So what do you think?"

Ethan wipes his hands on a rag as he shakes his head. "I have no clue if this quick fix is going to hold up or not and we don't have time to check the tie rods. If you got hit hard enough, they're probably bent and your whole steering is going to be fucked up."

"I guess we'll find out when we get it going." I glance over at Ella and Lila, laughing in the corner of the garage.

"You're not going to take her with you when you race, are you?" Ethan rounds the back of the car and starts checking the tire pressure.

"Not with the car running like it is."

"And what if she gives you a hard time."

271

"She won't." I check the oil. "At least I think she won't."

Ethan wipes his hands on his jeans. "I think that all depends on which Ella you're dealing with. The nice, polite one or the one who got you into this mess."

I look over at Ella again as she bends over to get a soda from the cooler behind the chairs. Her short shorts ride up and the bottom of her ass peeks out. After getting a drink, she drops back in her chair and opens it up, laughing at something Lila said. I adjust myself and slam the hood of the car down. "I think she might be a little of both."

***

"Why are there so many more people tonight?" Lila asks from the backseat, gaping at the cars parked up and down the road. "It wasn't this bad the last time we were here."

The girl is scared shitless and I kind of feel bad for her. "Mikey likes to draw a crowd."

"To watch him lose?" she asks, prodding Ella with her elbow.

"Maybe," I say with a heavy sigh, psyching myself out as I climb out of the car.

The three of them follow me out and Ella takes my hand as we hike through the crowd where Mikey's talking smack to some skater dude who drives a Honda in the middle of the crowd, showing off for everyone. There's a bonfire burning over near The Hitch and people sitting on tailgates, drinking beers, waiting for the race to start.

I push my way through the crowd, keeping a hold of Ella's hand. When we step out into the open, everyone looks at us and gossip starts flowing.

Mikey stops talking and claps his hands loudly. "Holy crap, I didn't think you'd actually show up."

"Do I ever not show up?" I say. "You're the one that backed out the last time we tried to race."

He spits on the ground and crosses his arms. "So which one of you's racing? The little one with the big mouth that got you into this mess? Or are you gonna race me yourself?"

Ella starts to move forward. "I'm—"

"I am." I squeeze her hand, pulling her behind me.

"Micha," she hisses. "This is my thing. I can handle it."

I shake my head, not looking at her. "Let's line up and get this over with."

Mikey grins, rubbing his hands together. "What? You eager to get your ass kicked?"

"No, I'm eager for you shut up." With that I turn away and head back to the car with Ella in tow.

"Micha Scott," she says, tugging on my arm and planting her feet in the dirt, trying to get me to stop walking.

Ethan and Lila are a ways back and Ethan's trying to explain to Lila the rules of racing. I keep walking forward, dragging her along with me, refusing to let her have her way this time—not with this.

"Stop being all noble and just let me drive," she says hotly. "It's much better for me to lose to him then for you to. He'll bug you about it for the rest of your life."

I stop just in front of the car and turn to her and brush the pad of my thumb across her cheek. "Hey, who said anything about losing?"

She gathers some strands of hair out of her face and stares at the front end of the car. The glow of the fire highlights the worry in her eyes. "I know Ethan and you didn't get everything fixed. You were working too fast and I'm sure you didn't do that great of a job."

"The car's fine," I assure her. "But you need to sit this one out."

"No way," she argues, folding her arms over her chest defiantly. "I'm going to at least sit in the passenger seat and ride with you. "

I shake my head. "Not this time, pretty girl." She starts to fume, so I lean in and kiss her right in front of everyone, cupping the back of her head and grabbing her ass, letting people know she's mine. Her body trembles as she kisses me back, even when someone whistles.

When I pull away, she has this glazed look in her eyes. "Now take Lila and go sit over by the finish line."

She opens her mouth, then seals her lips shut and nods. Ethan and her trade places and she walks off with Lila over toward the line.

Once they're out of sight, Ethan says, "You sure you want to do this?"

I nod, my gaze tracking the line of the road and the trees next to it. "You sure you want to do this?"

"Absolutely," he says. "I have nothing better to do."

We bump fists and climb into the car. I rev up the engine a few times, then inch it forward across the dirt and through the crowd toward the lineup area in front of The Hitch.

"How's the steering?" he asks rolling down the window, and letting the night air flow in.

I veer it from side to side, testing it. "It's shaky."

"Left or right?"

"To the right."

"Make sure you do your turnaround to the left then."

I nod as we roll up to the lineup and Mikey's already waiting for us. Ella and Lila are just off to the side, near the trees, sitting on the tailgate of someone's truck. She has her eyes glued to us as Lila talks to her, swinging her legs. I thrum my fingers on the top of the steering wheel, eyeing the end of the road.

"Quit psyching yourself out," Ethan says and snatches up the iPod. "I think it's time for a little tunes." He scrolls through the music and "The Distance" by *Cake* flips on. He cranks it up so the base is bumping and we start nodding our heads. When it hits the chorus we start singing and Ethan taps his fingers on the dash, like he's playing the drums. The more the song goes on, the more we get into it. I catch Ella laughing and shaking her head at us, because she knows this is Ethan and mines thing, but usually she's in the car with us.

"Hey, are we going to race?" Mikey shouts, slipping out his window and looking at us from over the roof with his hands in the air. "Or are we going to sit around and listen to music?"

I floor the pedal so loud the sound rumbles through the night and his eyes widen slightly. He gets back into his car and throttles his own pedal. It's half as loud and Ethan and I laugh at him.

"Dude, quit wasting time and get your girl over here to start us off," he calls out over the music.

I turn it down a notch. "Get Chandra to do it."

"No man, you know the rules," he says with a smirk. "The girlfriend of the one being challenged has to start off the race."

I roll my eyes, knowing Ella's not going to like this, the old or the new version. I slide out of the window, cup my hands around my mouth, and shout over the roof at her. "Ella May, get your beautiful ass over here."

Lila has her distracted and she jumps. Her eyebrows furrow as I wave her over. She holds up a finger to Lila and hops of the hood, looking at me perplexedly as she makes her way through the crowd and over to me. I sit back in the car as she reaches the window and she lowers her head down, looking into the cab.

"You have to start us off," I tell her and she instantly makes a face. "It's the rules. You know that."

"Those rules are sexist," she says. "Let Mikey's slutty girlfriend do it."

"You know he's not going to let that happen."

"I could make him let it happen."

I press my lips together as her spitfire personality burns through all her fake politeness. "Can you just do it for me?"

She rolls her eyes, then leans in and kisses my cheek. "But only for you."

Then she backs out of the car, with an exaggerated sway of her hips, making fun of the ordeal, but still looking hot as hell in her little shorts. Ethan and I bust up laughing as she turns around with a big embellished grin on her face.

"Well, at least she's entertaining," he says, patting the side of the door with his hand to the beat of the music.

I pump the gas a few times, my gaze attached to hers as she elevates her hands above her head. She looks at me as she counts down. When her arms drop, the tires squeal as we peel out.

Ella

I walk back through the cloud of dirt and hop on the tailgate with Lila. I spot Grantford through the crowd and when he sees me, he hurries away, ducking into the crowd, knowing Micha's around.

Lila swings her legs, taking in the surroundings. "What was that about?"

"Rules," I sigh, leaning forward so I can get a better view of the road.

It's hard to tell because it's dark, but it looks like Micha is winning. I start to grow restless the farther away the taillights get and I jump off the tailgate and pace the dirt.

"You're nervous," Lila observes. "And you're making me nervous."

I bite on my fingernails, unable to settle down. "I don't know what my problem is. Usually, I'm not this jumpy."

But I think deep down, I know exactly what my problem is. My feelings for Micha have been freed and now they consume me, own me, bind me to him. The crowd starts moving, nearly trampling me as they stare down the road, waiting for the turnaround. I hear the scared tones in their voices first before the crash. It's like a train wreck, metal crushing and snapping apart.

Lila's eyes snap wide. "What the hell was that?"

I spin around and shove my way to the front of the crowd. There are a few cars on the side backing up onto the road.

"Shit," someone says. "I think one of them wrecked."

I feel my heart crumble as I take off down the road.

"Ella!" Lila shouts. "Where are you going?"

I keep running, stumbling through the dark, searching for their lights. My flip flops fall off somewhere, but I keep going, needing to know. Cars are pulling out behind me and headlights shine at my back. Seconds later, Mikey's car zooms by and he shouts something foul at me.

Halfway down the road, the air turns to dirt and the sound of "The Distance" by *Cake* floods the air, only it's stuck and keeps saying the same line over and over again.

Spotting the outline of the car, I slow down. Suddenly, I'm back to the night my mom died. The Chevelle is smashed against the trunk of a large tree, the windshield smashed to pieces, and two of the tires are blown out.

279

Somehow it must have flipped around and the driver's side took most of the impact.

I know whatever's inside the car is bad, just like when I opened the bathroom door the night I found my mom and I won't be able to do anything about it. I almost turn away and run, not wanting to see it, but the passenger side door swings open and Ethan stumbles out, clutching at his upper arm. There's a path of blood dripping down his arm and his cheek is scraped.

I snap out of my own thoughts and rush to him. "Are you okay?"

"Ella, go get some help." He coughs, nearly buckling to his knees.

"No." My voice comes out sharp and high-pitched and vomit burns at the back of my throat. I gently push him aside and climb into the car, which is filled with dirt and the air is muggy.

"Micha." I cover my mouth and shake my head.

His head is flopped back against the headrest and turned away from me and his arms are slack to the side. Branches are poking in through the window and it looks like one of them might be lodged into his shoulder.

His head turns toward me and his eyes widen. "Fuck. Ethan, get her out of here."

280

Ethan reaches in to pull me back, but I climb onto the console, taking in the long, thin stick stabbed in his shoulder. I can't breathe. I can't lose him. I can't do this again.

"Ella May, look at me." His voice is hoarse as he locks eyes with me. "I'm okay, now back out of the car so Ethan can get me out of here."

My eyes scan his body, looking for any more wounds that could be hiding from me. "It's just the branch? That's the only place you're hurt?"

He nods lethargically. "A few stitches and I'm as good as new."

Kissing his forehead, I take a deep breath, hating to leave him as I back out of the car. Ethan's walking up the road toward me with Benny at his side. He's still clutching his arm and there's a little bit of a limp to his walk.

"Someone's got to have two good arms to pull it out," he says to Benny and I see him glance at me with concern in his eyes.

Benny nods and hops into the car, while Ethan and I wait impatiently on the outside. Cars start to pull up, headlights lighting up the accident as people rubberneck. One of the cars is a Camaro and Mikey stands in front of it, laughing with his girlfriend at his side.

"Fucking asshole swerved at us," Ethan tells me as he glares at Mikey.

Rage engulfs me and this time I let it take me over. I march up to him and shove him hard so he stumbles back into the front end of his car.

"You think this is funny?" I shout. "They crash into a tree because of you and you keep driving. What the hell's wrong with you?"

His eyes darken and he steps toward me. "I won and that's all that matters."

Shaking my head, I lift up my leg and knee him in the balls, hard. He groans, his face reddening as he hunches over and his girlfriend runs to his side to coddle him. I start to leave when he straightens back up. Cradling his injured guy parts, he charges, ready to hit me.

Ethan blocks him and shoves him back with his good arm. "If you touch her, I'll slam my good fist into your face."

This is not the first time he's had to say that to someone on my behalf.

Mikey backs down from the fight, muttering something about it not being worth it as Benny helps Micha out of the car. The branch is out of his shoulder. Left in its place is a hole, which is bleeding down his arm and shirt, but he's alive and breathing and that's all that matters.

We get him into the front seat of Benny's GTO and then Ethan and Lila get in the back. Micha has me sit on his lap, and he nuzzles his head into my chest. I hold onto him tightly as we speed off into the night.

Chapter 21

Micha

The hospital lights are bright and the air is a little cold, but Ella's warm hand in mine is comforting. The doctor doped me up with a sedative to ease the pain and then I lay down on the bed, waiting for them to come clean the fragments of the branch out of my wound.

I was scared shitless when I crashed into that tree, worried I was going to die and leave Ella behind with no one. But now, I'm feeling pretty good.

Ethan peers over me and scrunches his nose at the wound. "It's gnarly looking."

I shove him out of the way and pull Ella down beside me. "Hey there, pretty girl, come sit with me."

She giggles, then glances at someone and laughs harder. "I think you might be better off trying to shut your eyes," she tells me.

I shake my head from side to side. "No way, all I want to do is stare at you all day."

She snorts a laugh and then smoothes my hair back from my head. "Quit talking, before you say something embarrassing."

I search my brain, not finding anything embarrassing stashed away inside. "I'll be fine." I reach over with my good hand and find her leg. Grabbing hold of it, I pull her over toward me so she falls onto the bed.

"Micha," she says, her green eyes so wide I can see my reflection in them. "There are people everywhere."

I glance from left to right, not seeing anything but blurry shapes. "I think we're good." I move into kiss her and she gives me a quick peck on the lips, before leaning away.

"How about you rest your head in my lap," she says. "And I'll rub your back until you go to sleep."

"But what if I wake up and you're not here?" I ask, sounding like a little baby, but not giving a shit.

She presses her lips together and sighs. "I'm not going anywhere."

"You promise?"

"I promise."

She sits up and I rest my head on her lap. She rubs her fingers up my back and through my hair. I hold onto her as I drift into unconsciousness.

Ella

Micha is lying on my bed without a shirt on, fiddling with the bandage covering the hole where the branch stabbed into him. The doctors couldn't stitch it up because it was too wide of an injury, so he has to keep it covered and is not allowed to take showers, something he had jokingly griped about at the hospital as he winked at me.

It's been a few days since the accident and the Chevelle is parked out in his garage in ruins. When I saw it in the light, I practically passed out because it doesn't look like an accident anyone would walk away from; the driver's door is caved in and the front fender fell completely off.

"This is going to leave an awesome battle scar." He pushes the bandages back down over the wound.

"I'm glad you think so." I read the email that showed up in my inbox the day after the accident. Turns out, I got the internship at the museum and now I have no idea what to do. I want to do it—it's a great opportunity, but I also don't want to leave him.

"What are you reading?" he asks, sliding his legs off the bed, starting to get to his feet.

"Nothing. I was just looking through my emails." I shut the computer screen off, climb onto the bed with him, and lean back against the headboard, stretching my legs out.

He points at the drawing of the broken mirror on my wall. "I like that one. Especially the guitar part."

It turned out to be my best piece, full of memories, and a future I wasn't able to see until I finally let go. A freedom given to me by Micha because he refused to let me go.

"Me too," I agree. "I think I'll probably turn it in as one of my art projects one day."

"It's got a lot of meaning in it," he comments.

I smile and slide down, putting my head next to his. "I know."

He rolls to his side carefully, so he doesn't hurt his shoulder and we're lying face to face. "Where's your head, Ella May? Ever since the accident, you've been really quiet."

I'm so close to him I can see the dark specks of blue in his aqua eyes. I've been quiet because that night made me realize something important. For a split second, I thought I'd lost him and it opened up my heart and freed what I'd buried deep inside me that night on the bridge.

I look into his eyes, no longer afraid of what's in them, but afraid I'll lose what they carry. "I just don't ever want to lose you."

His eyebrows dip together as he props up onto his elbow. "Is that what it's been about? The accident? Because I'm fine." He points to the bandages. "It's just a tiny scrape."

"I know you're okay," I say, sounding choked. "But for a second I didn't think you were."

"Hey." He cups my cheek and kisses me tenderly. "I'm okay. You're okay. Everything's okay."

I take a deep breath and let it out before I can suck it back in. "Micha, I love you."

Chapter 22

Micha

She looks terrified as hell, her eyes round, and her body is trembling as she says, "I love you."

My smile breaks through. "I know you do. I have ever since the day on the bridge." She looks confused so I explain further. "When you tried to leave, I caught up with you and took you up to our spot by the lake to calm you down. When you did, you told me that you loved me."

Her lips part. "I did… why didn't you tell me?"

"Because I wanted you to tell me again," I say. "When you were a little less out of it. Took you long enough, by the way." Her lips expand to a smile and I can't help but kiss her.

My body rolls onto her on its own accord, even though it hurts like hell to use my arm to keep my weight off her. She trails her fingers up my back as her legs fall to the side, giving me permission to press up closer to her. It's what we've been doing every night for the last few days, almost reaching the end, but not quite.

Suddenly, she jerks back and I blink my eyes open. "What's wrong?"

Biting on her lip, she sits up and I lean back, giving her room as she slips her shirt and bra off and throws them on the floor. Locks of her auburn hair fall across her chest. Grinning, I move my lips for hers again, but she shakes her head and stands up on the bed, slipping her shorts and panties off and discarding them on the floor.

I've seen her naked a couple of times over the week — and once when we were sixteen and she left her curtain open — but each time gets my adrenaline pumping. She kneels down in front of me and kisses me passionately, her nipples brushing against my chest. Her body is shaking in a way that means she's nervous.

"Make love to me," she whispers against my lips.

I've been dreaming about those words leaving her lips since I was sixteen. "Are you sure?"

She nods with a sparkle in her eyes. "Yeah, I'm sure."

I wait a few seconds longer to give her time to back out if she needs to. She remains silent and reaches for my shirt, helping me pull it over my head so I don't have to lift up my arm. Her fingers run across my tattoo, lyrics I wrote about her, although I don't think she knows it. Then her hands find the button on my jeans and she unfastens it. Deciding to help her out, I peel my jeans and boxers off.

Grabbing a condom from my wallet, I lie her down and situate between her legs.

"Are you sure you're sure?" I check again.

Her auburn hair is spread across the pillow and the light above our heads reflects in her green eyes as she nods. "Micha, I'm more certain about this than I am about anything else in my life."

Suddenly, I get a little nervous. This is the first time I've ever been with someone I've cared about and it's going to be different.

Mentally preparing myself, I slide into her slowly so I don't hurt her. Her legs promptly constrict around my hips and she squeezes her eyes shut. I give her a minute, letting her breathe through the pain. When she opens her eyes again, I push into her further. Her head tips back as she forces air in through her nose. I start rocking in and out of her. The pained expression slowly turns to ecstasy and her eyes gloss over.

It's the most beautiful thing I've ever seen.

Ella

At first it hurts—more than I anticipated. I'm wondering what the big deal about sex is, when he starts rocking in and out of me, pushing in further and filling me with him. The pain eases away and all that's left is hunger.

I secure my legs around his hips and open up to him as his lips cover mine. He kisses me fervently and I start coming undone, releasing all control of my body and mind. I let my head fall back as he sucks and nips on my neck and down to my breasts, before returning his lips to mine. Our skin covers in sweat as his movements become harder, thrusting deeper inside me. I scream out his name as a fire inflames within me and everything comes apart. Moments later, his movements become jerkier and then he stills.

His head is tipped down and his warm breath caresses my neck. He places a kiss on my collar bone, then on my lips, finally looking at me and smoothing my hair back from my damp forehead.

"I love you," he whispers with a content expression.

I smile at him as he carefully slips out of me. Then he holds me in his arms and we drift off to sleep, relaxed and satisfied.

***

I wake up to Micha sitting on the bed in his boxers, playing his guitar, the tune "Behind Blue Eyes" by *The Who*. He's got his head tipped down as his fingers pluck away.

Sitting up, I rub the tiredness out of my eyes while holding the sheet up to cover my chest. "Why are you playing your sad song?" I ask.

He keeps singing, shutting his eyes, really getting into it. "It's not my sad song anymore." His fingers keep playing.

I tuck my legs under me and kneel up in front of him. "Since when?"

"Since the night you opened up to me," he says. "And it was playing over and over again. From now on, every time I hear this song, I'm going to think of you."

I shut my eyes and listen to him play a little longer, letting his beautiful voice flow over my skin. When he stops playing, I open them back up right as he yanks the sheet away from me. I scream and then laugh as he lays me back down and enfolds his body over mine. I kiss him passionately, giving extra attention to the ring in his lip.

"I have to tell you something," he says when I free his lip ring from my teeth.

The sound in his voice makes me uneasy. "Okay…"

He sighs and rakes his fingers through his hair. "I think I'm going to go on the road with Naomi and her band."

I sit up, shocked, and nearly bump foreheads with him. "Did she ask you to join?"

"Yeah, a few weeks ago, but I told her I had to think about it." He rolls to the side, bringing me with him and hitching my leg over his hip so I'm opened up and vulnerable to him. "I think this is something I have to do, otherwise I'll regret it for the rest of my life."

My mind is racing, but I force my voice to sound even. "When are you leaving?"

He traces my cheekbone with his finger. "In a couple of days."

Shutting my eyes, I talk myself through it. I know I have to let him go because regrets do nothing but eat away on the inside. It's still hard, though.

I force a small smile as I open my eyes. "Will you visit me in Vegas?"

"Every single moment I get," he says and seals his lips to mine. "I promise."

Chapter 23

Ella

We decide to visit Grady before we part ways and head off
on our separate adventures. Amy, his nurse, called me and
told me that Grady was still in the hospital, but that he
was allowed to have visitors. We make the hour drive
around the mountains and to Monroe Hospital, trying to
enjoy our last few days together.

It's a bright, sunny day, and the trees on the side of
the road are green. I hang my head out the window,
watching the road, feeling like there's so much waiting for
me in life.

"What are you doing?" Micha teases, turning the music down. "Trying to be a dog?"

I shake my head and look up at the bright blue sky.
"No, I'm just enjoying the nice, warm day."

He laughs at me and turns the music back up. My
head remains out the window until we reach town, then I

return to my seat. When we pull up to the hospital, blue and red lights light up the parking lot and my stomach constricts thinking about the night they showed up to take my mother's body away.

Micha squeezes my hand, letting me know he's there for me. "You ready for this?"

I nod and we walk hand-in-hand across the parking lot and through the automatic glass doors. A lot of people are sitting in the waiting room and there is a baby crying loudly on a woman's lap. The smell of cleaner collides with my nostrils as we walk up to the front desk where a secretary is talking on the phone. She's young with dark hair woven in a bun on top of her head. I catch her eyes skimming across Micha as she hangs up the phone and turns to us.

She overlaps her hands and sets them on the counter. "Can I help you?"

"Yeah, can you tell us what room Grady Morris is in?" Micha asks with a polite smile.

She taps her fingers on the keyboard and then reads the screen. "He's on the second floor in room 214."

We nod graciously and head for the elevator. Micha swings his arm around me, guiding me closer as we reach the floor and I slip my hand into the back pocket of his jeans, craving his comfort. When we enter the room, my insides twist until I notice Grady is sitting up in his bed, eating a cup full of green Jell-O. He looks pale under the florescent light, his arms nearly bones, and his eyes are more sunken in then the last time I saw him. A machine is hooked up to him, beeping in the corner, and an IV is taped to the back of his hand. Some of his items from home are hanging on the wall, making them not so bare.

Somehow, he manages to genuinely smile. "Just what I wanted. To see my two favorite people in the whole wide world."

I loosen up and Micha and I pull up chairs beside his bed on opposing sides of one another. Grady pushes the tray out of the way and sets his hands in his lap.

"So do you want to tell me what's up?" he asks and Micha and I exchange confused looks. "With the cuddly entrance you two made."

"Micha made me do it," I joke, sliding a glance at Micha. "He was being a baby. Said he needed to be coddled."

Micha winks at me. "Yep, and you fell for it."

Grady shakes his head and a frail laugh escapes his lips. "Ah, it's good to see you two back together." He grows silent, fixing his attention on me. "You look happier than the last time I saw you."

"I am happier," I tell him, resting my arms on his bed.

"You're still not there though," he says with concern.

"I know," I say. "But I'll keep working on it."

He seems content with my answer. "I have something for you over in the corner."

Micha and I track his gaze to a small box nestled in the corner of the room. I walk over to it and peer down inside. My smile expands as I pick up that broken vase I destroyed when I was a child. It's black, with a red pattern around the top, but the bottom is shattered out, so it can never hold flowers again.

I turn to him with the vase in my hands. "You kept this?"

He shrugs. "Just because it's broken doesn't mean it loses its importance. And I figured I'd give it to you one day when you realized it was okay to make mistakes."

Tears build up in the corners of my eyes. "Thank you, Grady. And I mean that. Thank you for everything. For giving me a small amount of comfort during my childhood and letting me know that not everything has to be difficult."

"You're welcome," he says simply.

I go over to the bed and hug him, trying not to cry, but a few tears slip out and I quickly wipe them away before I pull back.

We talk a little more about the stuff we're doing, then the nurse shows up and shoos us out so she can change his sheets. Micha and I leave, knowing it will probably be the last time we see him again. I cry the whole drive home, clutching on to the broken vase. But with Micha at my side, I know I'll be alright.

Micha

"Now are you sure you packed everything up?" My mom asks for the billionth time.

I never told her what happened with my dad. I didn't want her to have to worry more than she already does. That's one moment I'll keep locked away forever.

I pick up my guitar case from my bedroom floor and swing my bag over my shoulder. "Yes, I have everything packed, Mom. Now will you relax? You're driving me crazy."

"I'm sorry," she apologizes. "Oh wait. Do you have enough money?"

I shake my head. The woman's going to worry herself to death. "Of course."

Tears puddle in the corners of her eyes and she gives me a hug that nearly squeezes the air out of me. "Micha Scott you're the best son a mother could ask for."

I press my lips together, trying not to laugh at her overdramatic reaction. "I'm going on the road for a few months, mom, not dying."

She pulls away, wiping the running mascara underneath her eyes. "It doesn't mean I'm going to miss you any less."

"Yeah, we'll see if you say that after I'm back for a week and you're finding bras in your bed again."

She swats my arm and points at the door. "Okay, now you can go."

Laughing, I head out the back door. Naomi isn't here yet, so I sit down on the steps, staring at Ella's house, wondering if she's going to come out. She's never been good at good-byes so when her bedroom window slides open, I'm surprised.

But I'm even more astonished when she scales out of the window and down the tree. She has the sexy, strapless dress on, and her auburn hair is covering her bare shoulders. She doesn't say anything as she flings her arms around my neck. Her breath is hot against my ear and she buries her face into the side of my neck. I drop my guitar case and bag to the ground, pick her up, and embrace her with everything I have in me.

"I'm going to miss you," she whispers softly.

I run my hand up and down her back, shutting my eyes, and breathing her in. "It'll be okay. I'll be back and annoying you before you know it."

She looks at me with her big green eyes and then seals her lips over mine, kissing me indefinitely. My hands feel every part of her body, memorizing every curve, and the smoothness of her skin. I back us up against the tree into the shade, and slip my hand underneath her dress, feeling her there too.

"Alright Romeo, it's time to go." Naomi honks the horn of the SUV.

Sighing heavily, I release Ella and she puts her feet back on the ground. "I'll call you every day."

I kiss her one last time, then get into the car. She watches me the entire way down the driveway, with her arms folded, fighting to stay composed. When we turn onto the road she walks to the end of the driveway, keeping her eyes on me for as long as possible. But eventually we slip away from each other.

Chapter 24

Ella

"Are you sure you want to do this?" I ask Lila for the thousandth time.

She piles the last box into her trunk and slides her glasses over her eyes. "Hmmm... let me think. Go back to a home where I'm nothing but a burden? Or go back to the campus with you and have some fun?"

I pick some dirt out from underneath my fingernail. "I'm just making sure, before you get too committed."

She takes my hands and gives them a swing. "I want to go with you, okay, so go say good-bye to your dad so we can hit the road."

"Okay, I'll be right back." I head across the front lawn for the door when Ethan's truck pulls up in my driveway.

I walk up to his window and rest my arms on it. "So you got my message I take it?"

He looks like he just came from work, grease on his face and clothes, and his dark hair has some shavings of rust in it. "Yeah, I figured I'd come and say good-bye to both of you."

I slant my head to the side and pierce him with an accusing gaze. "Don't try and pretend that you're here for me."

He places his hand over his heart, faking hurt. "My heart is breaking and you're making jokes. Wow, you really are evil."

"Yeah, yeah," I back up so he can open the door and climb out. "I'll give you two a minute."

"I think you've overestimating what's going on between the two of us."

"Well, I wouldn't have to if one of you would tell me what's going on."

He shrugs and then rounds the back of the truck. Rolling my eyes, I walk into the house to tell my dad I'm leaving and that I plan on coming back in a couple weeks to meet up with Dean. After a long talk on the phone with him—and I'm sure a lot of persuading from Caroline—we decided to meet up here, when Dean can take off work, and give my dad an ultimatum. It's probably one of the hardest things I'll have to do, because I know there will be things said during the conversation that will hurt me. I'm going to push through it, though, because now I under-stand what I can handle.

I find him on the couch, eating a microwave dinner, with a six-pack on the table in front of him. He's watching the television, with a cigarette in his hand, and he barely notices me enter the room.

"Hey Dad," I say from the doorway. "I'm getting ready to leave."

He rips his eyes from the television, startled, and I wonder if he was even watching it or if he was dwelling in his thoughts. "Oh, okay, well drive safely."

I rub my sweaty palms together and walk into the room. "Dean and I are going to be coming back in a few weeks."

He sets his tray down and grabs a beer. "What for?"

I pat my hands on the sides of my legs uneasily. "We want to talk to you about something."

He sets the beer down. "I thought Dean was still here."

I shake my head, feeling guiltier about leaving. "He went home a week or two ago... but Dad, can you try and take care of yourself a little bit better?" I take a deep breath and throw a hint out into the open. "And maybe stop drinking so much?"

He glances at the row of beers in front of him like he just realized they were there. "Oh, I don't drink that much, do I?"

I sigh and sit down on the couch beside him. "You didn't used to, but now it's kinda all you do."

He bobs his head up and down. "Alright, I'll try to cut back."

I know he won't, but hopefully Dean and I will be able to convince him to go to rehab where he can get the help and counseling that he needs. I give him a hug, even though he winces. Then I walk away, hoping he'll be okay, but knowing that until he makes the decision to change all I can do is try to help him.

Epilogue

Ella

I've been back in Vegas for almost two weeks now and things are good. I signed up for some summer art classes and my internship at the museum is great, even though I spend most of my day cleaning up after people and running errands. I also started counseling. As much as I'd like to believe I was getting better, when I'm alone and lost in my own thoughts, the darkness sometimes gets to me. But my therapist is nice and the visits seem to be helping.

Lila is letting me borrow her car for the weekend, so I can drive back home and meet up with Dean and my dad. I'm glad to be making the drive alone, that way I'll have twelve hours to mentally prepare myself. Although, deep down, I wish Micha was going with me.

"Are you sure you don't want me to go with you," Lila asks as I clutch the handle of my suitcase and scan the room for forgotten items.

I shake my head. "I'll be fine and you have classes and your math tutor thing." I stop at the doorway, needing to get something off my chest. "Lila, thank you for letting me borrow your car and for just being there for me."

Her smile is bright. "Don't get all weepy on me. You're only going to be gone for a couple of days, silly."

We laugh, exiting the building and head down the stairs. Our apartment is right by the campus and we keep Lila's car in the parking lot most of the time. When we reach the grass that reaches across the campus, my phone starts to sing inside my pocket, a sad turned happy song.

"God, again?" Lila throws her head back dramatically. "Can't you two go five minutes without talking to each other?"

"No." I smile and answer the phone as Lila scoots away, giving us some privacy. "So how's the weather in Seattle?"

"Pretty sunny, actually," Micha says and I can hear the smile in his voice.

I jerk on my roll away bag as it gets caught in a hole in the lawn. "That's funny, because I thought it was supposed to be rainy there."

"Nope, I got a blue sky and a hell of a lot of sunshine over my head," he says. "And I'm really enjoying the view."

"Good, I'm glad," I tell him, missing him like crazy. "Are you still driving out here next weekend?"

"Actually there's been a slight change of plans," he answers. "And I can't come out next weekend."

I stop in the middle of the grass, pouting. "Oh. Okay."

He laughs softly into the phone. "You know, you're beautiful when you pout like that."

"How do you know I'm pouting?" I wonder.

"The same way that I know you have a sexy pair of shorts on and your hair is done up," he says and I start to glance around the campus at the people walking around in the quad and on the sidewalks. "Your ass looks really good, by the way."

I let my suitcase go and spin in a circle with the cell phone still to my ear. Then I spot him in the parking lot, standing next to a SUV in black jeans, a tight-fitted grey tee, and eyes as blue as the sky. I drop my phone and run to him, not caring that people are staring at me like I'm insane.

I don't slow down when I reach him and he catches me as I run into his arms. He picks me up and I secure my legs around him, kissing him with so much passion his lip ring cuts into my lip. Finally we pull back, panting with raw wildness in our eyes.

Jessica Sorensen

He tucks a strand of my hair behind my ear. "You didn't think I was going to let you go back home on your own, did you?"

"But you said you had to play this weekend."

"They can do one performance without me. This is more important."

I almost start to cry and he begins to panic.

"Ella May, what's wrong?" he asks. "This is a good thing, isn't it?"

"Yes, it is" I say, staring into his eyes. "I love you."

He smiles and whispers, "I love you, too," before re-connecting his lips with mine.

We kiss each other deeply, not caring that people are watching and whispering about us. To them we're just two people making out in the parking lot, creating a scene. They'll never really know what it took to get here. How many years were invested, but that's okay.

It's a secret between us.

Coming soon

The Forever of Ella and Micha (end of 2012)

The Temptation of Lila and Ethan (Winter 2013)

The Secret of Ella and Micha Playlist

1. *All the Same* by Sick Puppies
2. *The Story* by Brandi Carlile
3. *Shameful Metaphors* by Cevelle
4. *Rush* by Dance Movie
5. *Behind Blue Eyes* by The Who
6. *Black Sun* by Jo Mango
7. *Sail* by AWOLNATION
8. *The Distance* by Cake
9. *Live and Die* by The Avett Brothers

Acknowledgements

First off, I want to start out by giving a huge thanks to my husband for taking care of the kids and the house, while I locked myself away in my office, writing into the ridiculously late hours of the night.

And to my three kiddos, who make me smile every single day.

To Kristin Campbell and my mom, you guys are awesome. You read every single book I throw at you and help me improve them.

To my dad, who answered my questions about cars and told me the correct lingo.

And to my rock star of a cover artist, Regina Wamba, for making the best cover I could ask for.

Jessica Sorensen lives with her husband and three kids in the snowy mountains of Wyoming, where she spends most of her time reading, writing, and hanging out with her family.

Other books by Jessica Sorensen:
The Fallen Star (Fallen Star Series, Book 1)
The Underworld (Fallen Star Series, Book 2)
The Vision (Fallen Star Series, Book 3)
The Promise (Fallen Star Series, Book 4)

The Lost Soul (Fallen Souls Series, Book 1)

Darkness Falls (Darkness Falls Series, Book 1)
Darkness Breaks (Darkness Falls Series, Book 2)
Available May 23, 2012

Connect with me online:
http://jessicasorensensblog.blogspot.com/
http://www.facebook.com/#!/JessicaSorensensAdultContemporaryNovels?notif_t=page_new_likes
http://www.facebook.com/pages/Jessica-Sorensen/165335743524509
https://twitter.com/#!/jessFallenStar

2652781R00159

Printed in Great Britain
by Amazon.co.uk, Ltd.,
Marston Gate.